I0683189

ONCE UPON A TIME IN THE FUTURE

A. K. Kulshreshth

PRATHAM MANJARI BOOKS

First Edition © 2014 by A. K. Kulshreshth
Published by Pratham Manjari Books Pte. Ltd., Singapore, 2014
www.pratham-manjari.com

This second edition © 2018 by A. K. Kulshreshth
Published by Pratham Manjari Books, 2018,
Pratham Manjari Books is an imprint of Cernunnos Books Pte. Ltd.,
Singapore

The story 'The Examination' was published in *Mobius: The Journal of Social Change* (Summer 2013 issue).

This is a work of speculative fiction.
Any resemblance to real persons (living or dead) or organisations is purely coincidental. This book is intended for mature readers.

Illustrations by Su-Ann Oh and A. K. Kulshreshth

Literary editors: Desiree Ward and N. Henaff

Design and composition: N. Henaff

Cover illustration and design by Zoya Chaudhury
ISBN: 978-981-11-7323-3

A.K. KULSHRESTH'S short stories have appeared in literary magazines (including *Asia Literary Review* and *Wasafiri*) and anthologies in eight countries. Together with his mother, he has translated two novels (*Katora Bhar Khoon*, 1895 and *Chitralekha*, 1934) from Hindi to English, and is currently working on a third one (*Vaishali ki Nagarvadhu*, 1948-49). He has bachelor's and master's degrees in engineering, and a Ph.D. in management. He lives in Singapore and works in the technology industry.

Contents

Once Upon a Time

in the Future

TRUTH

THE EPIC *MAHABHARAT* tells, among other things, of the great war between the five good Pandav brothers and the hundred evil Kaurav brothers. Of course, even in this tale, good and evil are not neatly compartmentalised.

The five Pandav brothers were, in decreasing order of age, Yudhishthir, Arjun, Bheem, and the twins, Nakul and Sahdev. They did not know this, but their mother Kunti also had an illegitimate son, Karn, by the Sun god. Guru Dron was tutor to the Pandavs and Kauravs. Arjun was his star student and was being groomed to be the best archer in the world. A jungle tribal chief's son by the name of Eklavya secretly observed Guru Dron teaching Arjun, and subsequently became a self-taught archer. He considered Guru Dron his guru, though Dron had rejected him because he was a tribal. When the Pandavs found out that Eklavya was good enough to be a threat to Arjun, they complained to Dron. Dron asked Eklavya if he would accept him as a guru. When Eklavya confirmed this, Dron asked if he could claim his tribute, according to custom. Eklavya said that he could, and Dron asked Eklavya to cut off his right thumb and give it to him. Eklavya did so.

Later, Arjun won Princess Draupadi's hand in a contest. When the Pandavs reached their hut with Draupadi, Arjun shouted out to Kunti: 'Look, mother, what a treasure we brought for you.' Without looking, she replied that the brothers should share whatever it was. Because Kunti's word could not be disobeyed, Draupadi had to become the wife of all five brothers.

During the great war, Guru Dron had to fight on the side of the Kauravs though he loved the Pandavs in general and Arjun in particular. At a crucial point in the war, the Pandav strategy was to kill the guru by deceit because he was otherwise invincible. Dron was immensely fond of his son Ashwathama. Bheem killed an elephant named Ashwathama and shouted to Guru Dron that he had killed Ashwathama. Guru Dron said he would believe it only if Yudhishthir said so. Yudhishthir refused to do this, but the rest of the Pandavs thought of a workaround. Yudhishthir said, 'Ashwathama has been killed... Ashwathama the elephant.' When Yudhishthir delivered this news, the Pandavs drowned out the second part of the sentence with drums and cymbals. Guru Dron was disheartened, and he lay down his arms and went into a trance in his chariot, where a Pandav warrior beheaded him in this state.

The *Mahabharat* remains an integral part of Indian culture, religion, idiom and folklore. Tribal rights continue to be a complex issue in India, and this issue is linked to the current conflict in a large belt in Eastern and Southern India affected by the Naxalite movement. Polyandry is still practised (though it is declining) in pockets in Himachal Pradesh, a state in India near the scene of the *Mahabharat*'s action. When the epic was shown in a tacky serial on Indian TV in the late 1980s, life used to come to a standstill during its air time.

I

KNEW I WAS destined to be the Emperor, even then when I had only seen fourteen winters, but I did not mind losing the race to Arjun. Guru Dron was right: having Arjun on my side was better than having a thousand warrior princes. My knees hurt, my head throbbed, and the keen pain to the left of my solar plexus signalled that I had run as hard and fast as I could. Arjun overtook me with ease, even with the lotus clutched in his left hand. He increased his lead in rhythmic, controlled lunges as he leaned into the air, hungry to show the four of us how much faster he was. His back glistened with sweat. Our hut, in a corner of Guru Dron's gurukul, loomed into view as we passed a pipal tree.

'Look, mother, what a treasure we brought for you!' Arjun's voice was high pitched, and his words were punctuated with desperate gasps for air. We were still panting, all five of us. I mopped my forehead with my arm and looked back. The twins —Nakul and Sahdev—were many paces behind me and the lumbering Bheem, who weighed as much as all of us together, was huffing his way past the gurukul gate. We had just come from the lake three hundred steps away from the gate.

Before dawn broke, I had woken Arjun and the twins up. Then the twins had taken turns jumping on Bheem, to help me wake him up. Bheem got his revenge in the lake when he dunked them together in the water, one under each arm, for ten times. In between, he tickled them and made them laugh till they begged him to stop. Of course, he loved them too much to really punish them the way he punished some of Suyodhan's brothers. Bheem had a satisfied and vacant look as he floated on his back after that. There was a lull after all the screaming. Arjun was circling the lake shore, counting time and improving his speed.

I sat in the water on my favourite stone. Suyodhan and his brothers were away today. The lake was big enough for everyone, but I loved it when we had it to ourselves. It was the summer month of Baisakh, and this early in the day the water had only a feeble, soothing warmth. It reached my upper lip. I took in the sights and smells of the place which had been the starting point of our days for many mornings now. When we walked there by the light of the stars, the sky was still dark, and the dew had not yet evaporated.

The morning breeze carried the scent of moist earth to me. I could make out six different kinds of birdsong when I focused my mind on them. I had practised sharpening my hearing, and after a few cycles of the moon, I could deconstruct the harmony of the jungle sounds into individual melodies.

The sky had changed colour from a dark indigo to the palest of blues in those infinitesimal steps which we miss if we do not concentrate. I knew it would soon be time for us to run back so that we were not late for our class.

The rippling surface of the lake stretched for hundreds of stroke lengths ahead of me. Then there was the jungle, dark and ominous. As we became bigger and more proficient with weapons, my brothers and I were outgrowing our fear of the jungle and the Nishad people who had lived in it from the beginning of time.

I remembered the tense times when the Nishads had visited the gurukul, after the incident when Guru Dron had ensured that their prodigy, Eklavya, would not rival Arjun. With their matted locks and clothes made of bark, the Nishads had a ferocity which even I had found unnerving. I did not show it, but I was relieved when they left us in peace. I had never figured out how the tension was resolved. I did not ask Guru Dron, of course, because he could be a bit condescending, and the other elders seemed to clam up when I asked them.

Arjun interrupted my reverie. 'Brothers! Look!' he shouted. I looked to my left, toward the direction in which he had pointed.

It was beautiful. About a hundred strokes away to our left, amidst a flat mesh of large leaves, surrounded by lesser flowers, there was a beautiful blue lotus. It was small, but it looked divine in the breaking light.

'Brothers, what say we have a race?' Arjun said, slapping his muscular arms. He had the shine in his eyes that he got whenever he had a challenge to surmount. 'We swim to it, pluck it for Mother, and race back to give it to her. Whoever gets to her first wins...' he trailed off as he sensed my response.

We all knew who would win. He looked at me with a raised eyebrow. He knew I loved games of chance, even then.

'Or let's make it a bit unpredictable. Whoever gets there first plucks it. Everyone touches the plant. We swim back and dress. Then, we do the toss with the grass blades.'

This was a game I had invented. I had outgrown it, but the others hadn't. We would each pluck ten blades of grass. I would collect all of them, we would stand in a circle with our eyes closed, and I would throw the blades up in the air from the centre. The one who caught the largest number of blades was the winner.

'We run back to the hut in order of, you know. So, what do you say?'

'Hmm, I pondered.' I ran a palm over my wide forehead. I had been hearing compliments about how wide it was for as far back as I could remember. I said, 'We need to run back anyway. So, let's do it! Everyone, when I say now... Now!'

Bheem could have got to the lotus first—with his large lungs, he could get there without emerging to breathe. But he started too late. I guess I lost because I bothered to look at the others. I saw the flower being plucked when I was wading through the slush and plants surrounding it. It was Arjun. He grinned as we brushed past each other. I touched the stem, turned back, ducked smoothly past the other three and then dove into the deep water.

The lake was silent now, but the waters were choppy from our furious strokes. If we had known the outcome, we would still have struggled to win. Even the twins, whom we still treated like kids. It was in our blood.

When I got out of the water, I felt heavy and dizzy at the same time. My heart was pounding. I girded my loins tightly.

'Brother, you took my cloth!' Sahdev shouted to me. He was still breathing very hard through his mouth, his shoulders were heaving and his rib cage looked like it could split open any time.

'It doesn't matter. As long as Bheem gets his own,' I dismissed him. I checked that each of us had plucked the blades of grass. 'Here everyone, give me those blades.'

I collected the blades of grass. We formed a circle.

'Close your eyes, everyone,' I said. 'Hands outstretched, quickly.'

I threw the blades of grass up from the central point of our circle. When the blades came floating down, we closed our palms to catch them. Then we opened our eyes and counted. I had four, Arjun three, Nakul and Bheem two each and Sahdev none. I knew he would have sulked over it if he thought we had time to notice.

I started off, and Arjun followed as soon as I had taken my sixth stride. The flower would slow him a bit, but I knew he would overtake me soon. It was seventy strides before he did. I was happy about that. His bare feet landed softly, effortlessly on the earth, and his powerful legs propelled him ahead of me with every stride. Like me, he ran without kicking up too much dust. The shrubs on both sides blurred into streaks of green. On my right, I thought I saw a flicker, as if someone had darted through the green. I wondered who it could be, and then I cursed myself for not focusing on the one goal, as Guru Dron often taught us.

At the hut, Arjun shouted about the treasure to Mother.

'I don't need it,' she said. 'Be sure you share it equally, boys.'

Mother's words rang out. She stepped into the frame of the doorway. The lines on her forehead showed in the soft light. Sometimes—like last night—she got up with a start in her sleep. I stroked her forehead above her eyes, the way she used to stroke us, and helped her back to sleep. This morning, she had not yet had time to braid her hair, which fell about her in tangled, dark strands. She had stopped her maids from grooming her after Father's passing away. As always, she wore a single white cloth from shoulder to knees. She exuded such dignity that you would not need to be told that she was the Queen Mother. She looked divine to me.

Arjun had slowed down to avoid knocking mother over. He timed it perfectly. Like me, he was taller than her by now.

'We got it for you, Mother!'

He panted as he hugged her with one hand. With the other, he held the lotus high. Its blue stood out even more here, against the dull brown of our hut. Mother looked at the lotus but did not take it. Her face lit up and the lines on her forehead melted. She stood on her toes to kiss him between the eyes. The pain next to my solar plexus seemed to increase.

'Well, Mother has spoken, I said. I guess we have to share it.'

'How do we do that?' Nakul asked. He was hanging on to me for support. 'Let me keep it.'

'Hmm, I said. Arjun keeps it till noon, and then we take turns in the order in which we got here. Okay, everyone'

They all nodded, Nakul with the hint of a frown. It was too trivial to debate.

Mother looked toward the sun, which had just risen above the canopy of the jungle.

'Boys, you've almost stayed too long in the lake. Did you know Guru Dron is back? The lines were back on her forehead. He's meditating already. Do your breathing exercises. Quickly please? She patted Bheem, knowing he was likely to be the slowest one. He grinned. When you are done, go sit down at his feet, she continued. Be sure to be there when he opens his eyes, when the sunrays fall on him.'

We were in an irregular circle around her. Arjun still had an arm around her shoulder, and Sahdev had latched on to her as well.

'I wish we had more time,' Sahdev said. 'He still looked a bit cross. He couldn't say that he wished the guru hadn't come back a day early.'

'The Sun will not wait, dear. Don't waste any time now.' Mother was never cross, but she could be emphatic.

'A-ah, why doesn't the Sun take a break? Stupid one,' Sahdev said.

Mother flinched. I wondered why. She gave Sahdev a steely look. He was about to break into a sulk. He pointed at me, and I knew he was going to say something about the cloth. She softened and drew him to her bosom, kissing him on the forehead and stroking his matted and damp hair. Sahdev beamed like he did when he got an extra sweet.

'All life depends on the Sun,' she said. 'We never insult him. Is that clear?' Sahdev nodded with his lips pursed. 'Now boys, do the breathing exercise and off you go,' Mother said.

She turned to look at Bheem, who was caressing his belly, and sighed.

'Yes, Bheem, before you ask, there will be enough to eat after the lesson.'

Arjun and I laughed.

'Now, she continued firmly, not one word more. You'll be late!'

We had settled down in the classroom a few moments ahead of time. Arjun kept the lotus next to him in a jar of water. We were noiseless as far as we could make out. Guru Dron sat in the lotus position on the edge of the mud platform which was two hands high. He was clad in only a saffron-coloured loincloth. Next to him was a large cloth bundle. I wondered why it was there. His body was stiff, but his face was completely relaxed. His gray hair was tied neatly into a bun. His long, gray beard was tussled by the breeze and a few of its strands drooped to his hairy chest.

Only yesterday, Nakul had asked me when he would get hair on his chest like me. I told him it would be a few more winters. Then he wanted to know when he could shave his chin like he had seen Father do many winters ago. I told him it would be still more winters.

The guru opened his eyes and gazed on Arjun.

'We shall talk about…' he pondered. His voice was soft, almost a whisper. But each word was clear.

'Arrows? Archery?' Arjun asked. Guru Dron smiled.

'Is anything more important?'

Arjun frowned.

'I don't think so.'

The guru looked at me. I thought hard.

'Perhaps when to use them and when not to use them?' I said.

'Yes!' The guru smiled. 'Know this, because it is most important: the best war is no war! He scanned all of us as he spoke. You will master the use of arrows, swords and clubs as you are doing now. Only when you become skilled in these, you will learn to use them while riding horses, chariots and elephants.

You will learn the formations—the basic four, then the thirty-two. But only some of you will learn how to make a Chakravyuh formation. And only one of you— he looked at Arjun—will be good enough to break it!'

Arjun inhaled and straightened his back.

'But above all,' Guru Dron continued, 'you must know when to use your head, and when to use your arms.' We digested this.

'Will you teach us now?' Sahdev asked, breaking the silence.

The guru smiled.

'It can never be taught. Remember, you are princes. When you go to war, thousands will die. Why, then, should you learn the art of war?'

Sahdev shrugged.

'Because we want others to die—not to die ourselves.'

Bheem burst out laughing. The guru looked sternly at him, and he choked back his laughter.

'You choose the wrong words. Our first duty is to righteousness, to Dharm.' The guru made that gesture of his, in which he spread his fingers like a flower. 'We only fight to preserve Dharm. Having done this, we fight to win! Not to lose!'

Bheem nodded and looked serious.

'So, take this to heart: prakasayudh, open and scheduled war, which I now teach you to excel at, is only one way of war. There are three others which take fewer lives: mantrayudh, the clandestine war; kutayudh, war by deceit; and gudayudh, war by diplomacy. Other elders will teach you a bit about them, and life will teach you the rest.'

Nakul joined his palms in a namaste.

'Yes, Son, ask,' the guru said with a smile.

'If we build a big wall, much bigger than this one, Nakul pointed to the wall of the gurukul, isn't that the best way to keep our enemies out? Then we don't need any kind of war.'

Bheem laughed again, and then froze as he realised the guru was looking at him sternly.

'Do you know what wrong you committed?' Guru Dron asked Bheem.

'Yes, Sir. It took him a while to gather that he was expected to be more precise. I laughed at a question, and no question should be laughed at.'

'What would you suggest as a punishment for yourself?'

Bheem looked a bit sullen. A peacock crowed, twice, piercing the quiet.

'A thousand push-ups?' Bheem asked hopefully.

Guru Dron started to speak, but his voice was drowned out by a third cry from the peacock. He waited for quiet before continuing.

'Hmm. That might be a punishment for some of us. But for you—no. You will calculate the number of sunrises to go before the next eight changes of season. I was planning to do that myself later this day.'

He seemed quite satisfied with the punishment he had prescribed.

'I shall do so,' Sir, Bheem said, doing a namaste.

'Excellent! said the guru after a pause. Now, if I think about Nakul's question, let me try to answer it this way.'

He got up with a certain air. We knew he had something special to show us. He bent toward the cloth bundle beside him and pulled it away to reveal two swords: one of the ordinary kind and the other a shining sword, three arms long. It was of a brightness I had never even imagined.

He looked at us with a satisfied grin. It was rare to see him display such obvious pride.

'I worked with the jungle people over three winters to get this mix of the elements. A sword such as this can only be made from material deep in the jungles of Magadha, which can be reached after a journey of sixty-four sunrises, and at a risk to your life.' He pointed to Nakul. 'Now you, Nakul, take this old sword and try to stab my chest with it.'

Nakul stood up, a bit wary. His shoulders were slightly hunched. He walked over, climbed on to the platform, picked up the old sword and took up the stance. He knew better than to thrust halfheartedly.

'Now!' The guru shouted.

Nakul cried out and thrust with all his might. The guru sidestepped him and wielded his sword in a circle. All we saw was a shining blaze, and then there was a loud clang. Nakul was nursing his shoulder, and his sword was broken in two.

We knew we must not clap. We exhaled at the same time, all of us.

The guru patted Nakul.

'Sit down, Son, and tell me what you learned.'

Nakul was looking at the broken half of the sword in his hand thoughtfully when he sat down.

'It seems, master, that with this new material, we can get wonderful strength.'

'Not with the material!' The guru said. 'He was still flushed. First, we apply our mind. We make new weapons. And we have the strength of our bodies. We win the affection of our people with Dharm. Do we need a wall?'

'No, Sir,' replied Nakul, 'a wall may even stop those we want from coming in.'

The guru smiled.

'Exactly. We must be strong, we must be liked. Then we do not need walls. A wall such as this—he gestured to the wall behind us—is only to stop animals from straying in. No unwelcome man dares to enter the gurukul of Dron!'

That was when we heard the shrieks. Through the doorway, I saw that Kripi mata, Guru Dron's wife who was like a second mother to us, was running past the well toward us. She ran clumsily, her arms flailing and her breasts heaving. In a few moments, she was up there on the platform with the guru, kneeling beside him, wide-eyed and trembling. She clasped his upper arm, and her fingers dug into it. Guru Dron maintained his calm, and looked into her eyes.

'What is it?' he asked in a steady voice.

She opened her mouth to speak but no words came out, only breath. She had closed her eyes now and she was shuddering. She pulled herself together and tugged at the guru's arm. He seemed to realise she would not speak just yet. He got up and motioned us to follow them.

The guru took long strides to keep pace with Kripi mata as she ran. The sun was out in strength by now, and it took me a few moments to get used to its blinding light. Kripi mata led us to the space between the staff houses and the store.

The sight there should have filled me with horror, but I was only numb. It was the guru's assistant, Ugna. An axe was still embedded in his bare chest, and his skin was splattered with blood. The handle tilted to his left thigh. He was surely dead, beyond even the guru's powers of healing. His face was contorted in an expression which I could not describe then, and I do not want to now. He was clean-shaven as usual, and his mouth was agape. A trickle of dark brown blood had oozed out from it and solidified.

II

OUTSIDE, THE SHADOWS had grown longer. We were in Guru Dron's hut, where he had summoned us brothers, Mother and Kripi mata. He had asked one of the other students to take care of his son Ashwathama. We sat on the ground in silence for a long time. Kripi mata sat on Guru Dron's left, huddled and still visibly shaken. At intervals, she mumbled to herself. Mother sat on his right. She had that inscrutable look which she could put on at will.

I looked at the blue lotus in the jar, near the pillar where Arjun had left it. If it hadn't been for the murder, we would have had the lotus on our minds all day. Nakul or Sahdev would have quarrelled over it. Now it lay there, forgotten. I looked at Guru Dron and noticed for the first time that his temple was throbbing. He interlocked his fingers above his head and stretched himself.

'I was out for two days and one night, he said. It is unimaginable that this could happen. As you know, there has been a murder. He was becoming louder now. Ten silver pieces have been stolen from the Queen Mother, Rajmata Kunti's hut.'

Mother had told us about this only a short while back. We were silent. Guru Dron had looked straight ahead, but his words seemed to lash Kripi mata. I tried not to look at her. A peacock's crow broke the silence. A loud crow, and after fixed gaps, two more.

Guru Dron continued.

'Someone here has something to do with it. That shocks me. I cannot accept this—that things I do not understand should happen in my gurukul.'

He looked at all of us, one by one, starting with Arjun, moving to me, Bheem, Nakul, Sahdev, Mother and finally—longest and hardest—at Kripi mata. His gaze was steady, and Kripi mata seemed to flinch.

'There is a reason why I have not called the other students here. There is a secret being hidden from me, and at least one of you knows about it. I ask you, because my life and happiness depend on it. Who is it? What has happened? What is this about? Speak now!'

His lips twitched. He took a deep breath to control himself.

'I shall hear you patiently, he said, and judge you lightly. But if you hide anything from me, I shall get to the bottom of this. That is a promise.'

There was a long silence. Kripi mata started to regain her calm. Was she relieved about something? I remembered the shape in the jungle as we had run back from the lake that morning, and then a fleeting memory came back to me. When I had been half-asleep last night, I had heard two voices whispering loudly. I could not place them. They had almost been drowned out by the hum of the insects, but they had stood out enough. I knew from our training that a whisper can travel farther than we think. My attention wandered to the lotus again. I was tempted to reach for it.

'I am talking to you!' I was startled to see Guru Dron looking straight at me. Of course, he would. I was the eldest.

'Forgive me, Guru,' I said.

'I want to hear what you think,' he said to me, 'before I tell you all what I already know.'

'I do not know, Guru.'

'That is not what I asked you.' Guru Dron's voice was steely.

I kept calm, as a prince should.

'Forgive me Guru, but I do not even know what to think. I can summarise these facts: Ugna has been murdered outside his hut, ten steps behind yours. The handle of the axe buried in his chest tilted toward his left thigh.'

I noticed Arjun hanging on to every word, nodding to encourage me.

'The angle of the handle showed that the killer was taller than Ugna,' I continued. 'The killer was quick and efficient. He acted before Ugna could raise the alarm. And ten silver coins have been stolen from Mother's bronze box. I understand the coins were last seen three mornings ago.'

'And how easy would it be for a stranger to enter the gurukul?' Guru Dron asked, stroking his chin.

I looked out the windows on Guru Dron's right. I could see the pipal tree next to the well through one of them. I longed for the comforting coolness of the mud platform below the tree. I traced the layout of the gurukul in my mind.

'This wall, I said, almost as high as an elephant, is difficult to jump. It is almost impossible for a stranger to enter the gate any time during the day. After sunset and till sunrise, there is a student keeping watch at the gate.'

'And what else is relevant?' Guru Dron asked.

I looked down at my toes. They were caked with mud. My nails were overgrown and dirty. I had postponed trimming them for too long. I tried to order my thoughts.

'Ugna was last seen by Nakul last evening, just after sunset, when he was taking the cows into their shed,' I said. 'Today he was killed before he took them out to graze.' I looked at the guru. 'You arrived at the gurukul after sunrise today, one morning earlier than you had planned.'

I wondered about the movement in the jungle that morning, and the whispers the night before. Should I talk about them? How would it help? How sure was I about them? What might they mean? It was unsettling to even think that Mother or Kripi mata might have something to hide.

Guru Dron stroked his chin again.

'That is a good summary, if a bit disorderly. In this closed gurukul, someone came in on the very night when I was away. Someone murdered Ugna between last evening and this morning. Someone stole the coins.'

I looked at my brothers. Arjun was deep in thought. Bheem had that passive look of his, which gave him an undeserved reputation for being slow. Nakul and Sahdev sat with their chins cupped in their hands.

'Now, listen to this,' Guru Dron said. 'I had taught Ugna to tie a very thin thread across the gate. The thread was tied just above the height of the tallest among you—Arjun. I had told Ugna to tie one every evening, after locking the cows, and break it himself the next morning. The strand is still there, meaning that no one taller than Arjun left or came in from the gate!'

The hall was quiet. I took a deep breath. The hot air smelled of baked mud and hay. Mother sat there with her stony face. Kripi mata was calmer now, but

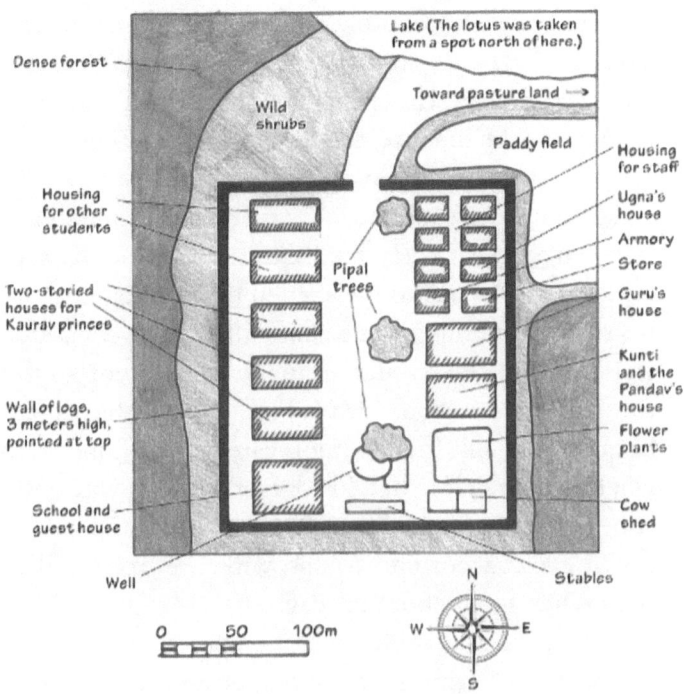

Lake (The lotus was taken from a spot north of here.)

Dense forest

Toward pasture land →

Wild shrubs

Paddy field

Housing for staff

Housing for other students

Ugna's house

Armory

Store

Pipal trees

Two-storied houses for Kaurav princes

Guru's house

Kunti and the Pandav's house

Wall of logs, 3 meters high, pointed at top

Flower plants

School and guest house

Cow shed

Well

Stables

0   50   100m

N W E S

Rough sketch of the Gurukul

her face fell for a moment. A drop of sweat plopped from my right armpit. My brothers' eyes were on the guru. Bheem's jaw had dropped.

'So,' Guru Dron continued, 'no one entered the gurukul by day or night, and yet we have a murder and a theft to explain. Let me tell you also that the tilting of the axe handle toward Ugna's left thigh might mean that the person who killed him was lefthanded.'

His voice almost broke as he ended, but he stayed calm. He gazed down toward the floor with a vacant look. Kripi mata was lefthanded, but surely that was not relevant to the case. On the other hand, there was something she had been uncomfortable about.

'Now, I will summarise everyone's movements as they have been told to me,' Guru Dron said. 'Ugna took the cows back to the shed in the evening. Nakul heard him humming while taking them. The cows are still in the shed. In the morning, Ugna did not go to the gate to break the thread as I instructed him, because it is still there. I took care to duck under it when I came in. He had his dinner with his wife and son, a little after sunset. He ate well, and slept not-so-well, according to his wife. He rose early, before her, to go about his day.'

He nodded to Arjun, who had raised his hand.

'Guru-ji,' Arjun said, 'if you permit me, I can try to see if there are any strange footprints near the gate.'

'It's no use,' Guru Dron said. 'There are too many of them. But that was a good thought.' Arjun's chest swelled a bit.

'Anyway, to continue, Kripi cooked dinner for Ashwathama and herself as usual while the shadows were lengthening. She went out to fetch water from the tank near the well, where she spent some time alone. Apart from that she has been by Ashwathama's side all the time. She and Ashwathama had dinner together and slept early. She was awake when I came home in the morning. She offered to wash my feet. Instead, I decided to go straight to the school. She told me that she went to the store after that, and she happened to see Ugna's dead body. She fainted at the sight, and when she came to, she ran to call us.'

The image of Kripi mata running into our class drifted into my mind. I looked at her now, sitting there pensive and forlorn, and wanted to reach out and comfort her.

'Rajmata Kunti and you boys had dinner when you five got back from your exercises of the evening. She was with you, watching you doing them. You, he pointed at me, went to the cowshed after you were done, while your brothers went home. You checked that the cows were all there, and then did a round of the gurukul. Then you joined the others for dinner. After dinner all of you were together. You repeated the sixty-four verses I had assigned and went to sleep.'

He took a long breath and focused his gaze on me. It struck me that you could never hear the sound of his breath, even after he had demonstrated the most strenuous physical exercises.

'Is this correct?' He waited.

There was that uncomfortable silence.

'Then, one of you has missed out something! His voice was level, only a bit louder than usual. But it was enough to startle us.'

He stared at me.

'You! Speak now and tell me if you saw Kripi sitting by the well in the evening!'

I knew then that I would never forget the look on his face, or the grief on Kripi mata's. His anguish came through in his voice and the strain of keeping his anger in check betrayed him. His right temple was throbbing again. Thankfully he turned his gaze away from me and fixed it so that it became vacant. Kripi mata's eyes had widened. I sensed mother's gaze on me and my eyes locked with hers. She had lost her stony look and was trying to tell me something without mouthing it. They were both begging me to just say the right thing.

A scene from the fringes of my memories occupied my mind. I was much smaller then. Kripi mata was carrying me after I had fallen and hurt myself. My tears dried as I felt her softness, warmth and strength. She patted me after she applied turmeric paste on my bleeding forehead, knees and palms. She stroked my forehead and said with a dimpled smile that the Pandavs were lucky to have me, with my wide forehead, leading them.

Now she sat here, frail and crumpled. I knew I must protect her. My breath became jagged, but I calmed it. The peacock cried again. I sensed that it was a signal for what I must do.

I counted till it was time for the peacock's second cry. I lowered my head.

'It is not true that,' I mumbled, knowing those words would be drowned out by the peacock. 'I saw Kripi mata sitting by the well, alone by herself,' I continued more firmly as I looked at the guru.

My word was enough.

It was worth more than everyone else's put together. In the silence, I felt my brothers' stares and sensed the relief Mother and Kripi mata felt. Guru

Dron pondered this, stroking his chin. A film of sweat covered his torso.

I had been doing my own thinking, and I thought I knew what had happened.

'Forgive me, Guru, I said, but I would like to add some observations.'

Guru Dron sighed.

'Of course, go ahead.'

'If I understand right, the problem is this: we think no stranger entered or left the gurukul. And yet there was a theft and a murder. To me, this makes it clear that we think wrong: someone did enter, and that someone also left.'

Guru Dron rotated his head once, with his eyes closed.

'Firstly, Sir, about the thread. I remember following Arjun's form when he ran past me today. He does not run while standing erect, no man can. I expect that if someone was running out of the gurukul, even a man as tall as Arjun and strong enough to kill Ugna, he would not break the thread.'

The guru's face softened.

'Continue, he said. Is there anything else?'

'Just this, Guru, that the person who killed Ugna must have been strong enough to do it cleanly in one blow. Also, as you have taught us, a right-handed person can swing the axe from his left if that is where his opponent is, relative to him.' Guru Dron nodded.

'It appears that someone—probably a Nishad— was brave, foolish and lucky enough to enter the gurukul in the evening and steal the coins from our house. He could have done this when we were doing our exercises, if the student who was on guard at the gate was slack. The other way to get in would be to catapult over the wall, though that is very unlikely. It appears that he had to hide behind one of the huts, and then run away in the morning. I cannot figure out how I did not see him, for example, when I did my round. But it is possible that in my subconscious mind, when I did the round, I did not seriously consider that there might be someone hiding. This is an important lesson for me.'

'And for the rest of us,' Guru Dron interjected. He pointed his finger at me. 'Go on.'

'In the morning, he was lucky to miss you and us—and Ugna had the misfortune of running into him unarmed. I should add that when we were running back, I thought I saw a man running through the jungle.'

My heart was hammering at my chest as I said all this. I knew I had no business to mention the movement in the jungle but leave out the whispers I had heard at night.

I could not tell who was more relieved, Guru Dron or Kripi mata.

III

I SAT ON THE mud platform under the tree next to the well. The shade of the tree covered the baked earth, but it still exuded waves of heat. The platform was much cooler. I had not eaten that day, and nothing would make me eat. I had not been able to do the exercises in the evening. I had the jar with the lotus with me. After I took it from Arjun, the others had forgotten to ask me for it. Or maybe they knew I did not want to be disturbed. It was only now, after many hours, that I almost felt at peace again as I willed the toxins out of my system. There was so much to ponder.

In the distance, Guru Dron carried Ashwathama on his shoulders. He would probably be teaching him to work with numbers, and when the stars came out, he would teach him their arrangements.

The cremation had been performed, and Ugna's wife had decided to stay on in the gurukul on Guru Dron's request.

Kripi mata headed toward me. I had wanted to have a chat with her. The pale saffron of her cloth glowed in the soft twilight. I stood and bowed my head as she drew near.

She sat down on the mud platform and clasped her hands, straining her knuckles. She reached for my hand, drew me toward her and I sensed that she wanted me to sit down. I felt tears trickling down my cheeks. They were warm. I was furious. I thought I had seen the last of my own tears many full moons ago.

She looked at me with a start and drew me to her shoulder. I felt a relief. My strength came back to me. It had done me good to cry a bit.

'I want to thank you for being wise,' she said.

'I followed my heart, Mata,' I replied.

'I know. I only want to say that you need not feel tormented. If you had not said what you did, the consequences would have been immense. And I want you to know what happened. Have you guessed?' She looked composed now. A flight of birds descended noisily into the tree.

'Does it have to do with Eklavya?'

'Yes.'

'His family demanded compensation?'

'Yes. His mother approached me through a messenger. I tried telling them that the guru could have imposed a much stricter punishment, that he had been lenient. He would have rejected the idea of compensation, and he will even reject me if he finds out what I have done. But I talked to Rajmata Kunti, and she agreed with me. She stroked my forehead. For your mother and you five to survive, you must choose your battles. You cannot afford this dispute.'

'And Arjun must become the best archer, I pointed out. Whatever it takes.'

'Whatever it takes.' She nodded.

'How did the Nishad get in?' I asked. 'Between the cows?'

'Yes,' she said. 'We thought it was the only way. We could not step out ourselves without attracting attention.'

'And what was the plan for his escape?' I saw her looking at the lotus. I would have given it to her, if it hadn't been for Mother's directions.

'I hid him in the store,' she said, 'and told him I would open the door at dawn. He had to make his way to the area behind the staff quarters. As soon as the student on duty rose, provided the Nishad did not hear you boys approaching, he was to dart across the gate into the shrubs. If something went wrong, he would come back and hide in the store. I thought I could manage things so as to involve no one else.'

'Fate was cruel to Ugna,' I said.

She hesitated.

'I cannot imagine a more pointless death, Son, but...' She sighed and lowered her head.

'He was in the wrong place at the wrong time.'

'Yes,' she whispered.

'Did you see the murder?'

'No!' She spoke louder, then continued softly. 'I left Ashwathama sleeping and went to open the store. I was jittery—your guru-ji had arrived early. The Nishad was ready to run. I thought everything would be fine, but I waited in the store in case he needed to run back. And then I looked out of the window and saw that sight. Like a fool, I took a long time to figure it out. Then I fainted. You know the rest.'

'Did you tell the Guru about the theft to create a motive?'

'Rajmata Kunti suggested that.'

'Mother knows everything?'

'Of course.'

'Are you sure you needed to keep all this from Guru Dron?'

'Yes. He would never accept the idea that he did wrong, and even the thought of compensation would be anathema to him. You don't know how relieved he is that you supported the idea of a Nishad thief.'

'I wish Mother had told me,' I said. The lines on her forehead increase every day as she pretends to be calm.

'She is very strong.'

'I still worry that I tricked the Guru, even if I did not violate Dharm.'

She stroked my forehead. 'I know, Son. Look at it this way: it happened once—it will never happen again, right?'

'Of course,' I said.

'We were very sure, Rajmata and I, that we were doing the right thing. And look where we all ended up—lying to the guru himself, and getting you involved in all this. At least we know it ends here.'

She motioned with her hand, and I gave her the jar. She admired the lotus from close, and returned it to me. She was still grave, but she exuded calm now.

'I will leave now, Son. You share our burden. I wish you did not have to bear it, but it is as much a part of growing from boy to man for you as your study and training. There is no choice.'

'You are right, Mata, there is no choice,' I said.

She smiled back wanly, planted a kiss on my forehead and got up to leave.

I lay on my back on the mud. A flock of glowworms lit up the darkness. The cool breeze carried the scents of the jungle past the wall into the gurukul. I again focused my hearing and separated the complex layers of sound which blended into the drone of the jungle. The hum of the insects was punctuated by the hoarse calls of frogs. I realised I had got my calm back. My eyes wandered past the thick branches of the tree, its sparse leaves reaching for the gray night sky.

And then I saw a pair of wide-open eyes looking down at me from the branches. Anyone else would have screamed.

It took me a few breaths to compose myself. It was Nakul. 'You monkey, get your butt down here!' I hissed at him, sitting up.

He jumped down from the tree, landing agilely on all fours. We looked at each other. He was still on his palms and toes, looking at me to see if he needed to run away. I knew it would be inappropriate to let him go.

'How long have you been here?' I hissed at him again.

'Longer than you,' he replied. His face broke into that smile which made it difficult for me to whack him.

'What were you doing up there?'

'I like it here. And then when you arrived, I wanted to stay with you, but I didn't want to disturb you.' He was still on all fours.

'And what about your dinner?'

'I don't feel like eating. Like you.'

'You monkey.' I realised I was running out of things to say. 'Now snap out of that silly position. Press my legs and shoulder for me, please. I am tired.' That would give me time to think.

'As you command, Brother.'

I relaxed as Nakul kneaded me, but the time I had gained didn't help me much. It was a pity, but he would have to bear his share of the burden.

'That was good, Nakul,' I told him. 'Now let's go. But before that, touch my feet and promise me you will not talk about any of this with anyone. I mean not even Sahdev.'

'About what?' he asked.

I twisted around and stared at him. His eyes sparkled, but the sparkle died down quickly when our eyes locked.

'I know,' he said.

'What?' I asked.

'Why Ugna was killed. One of them, the Nishads, came here to take money from Kripi mata. Ugna caught the Nishad while he was running out, and the Nishad killed him.'

'And do you know why we must keep this quiet?'

'Yes, Brother, I heard everything.'

'Why?'

'Because you said it.' He was dead serious now.

'True enough. As you heard, we have to choose our battles. Now promise me.'

He touched my feet, and then stood erect before me. He was already as tall as my chest.

'I promise you,' he said. I knew he would not betray the code of the Pandavs.

I patted his arm and said, 'Let's go.' I saw him eyeing the lotus. 'Pick it up, and keep it,' I said. He grinned and picked it up. Its blue had taken on a softer hue in the gloaming.

'Brother?' Nakul said.

'Yes?'

'You must be feeling better now. Won't you carry me there?'

I laughed.

'Climb on.'

I lowered my shoulders, and he sprang onto the platform and upon my shoulders in two neat steps. I tottered a bit when I stood up.

'Are you all right, Brother?'

'Yes,' I grunted. It would not be many winters before I would find it difficult to carry him. By the time we got to the hut, I was panting a bit and couldn't wait to hit the floor.

'Is it you both?' Mother whispered. She sat hunched on her bed, with her back against the wall. Her tired eyes were wide open.

I tiptoed over to her, hugged her and put a finger on her lips. 'I'm fine,' I whispered. 'And sleepy.'

She hugged us without a word. Nakul went off, treading with exaggerated softness, to occupy a part of the place the other three had left for us on the floor.

I pushed Mother's shoulders gently and got her to lie down. I stroked her forehead with my thumb and middle finger. When her breaths became deeper, I went over to my corner.

Nakul and I lay next to each other on the floor. I traced the outline of my forehead with my thumb. Kripi mata was the one who had always talked about how wide my forehead was, and how I would grow up into a wise man. How wise had I really been today? What else could I do when they thrust me into that situation? I realised that sleep would elude me for some time.

'Brother?' Nakul whispered.

I sighed and turned to him. 'What is it?' I whispered back.

'How do you know what is the right thing to do?'

I thought about it, taking my time. 'I am Yudhish-thir,' I shrugged and told him.

I wondered if that sounded arrogant. It was true, though. I waited for him to reply. Then I realised he must have been satisfied with the answer. His breath was steady. He was asleep.

THE TRIAL

THE LAST CHAPTER of the *Mahabharat* describes the last journey of the five Pandav brothers and their common wife, Draupadi.

During their journey, they were joined by a dog. As they climbed up the Himalayas, Draupadi was the first to fall, followed one by one by all the brothers except Yudhishthir, who was the most virtuous. The god Indra came to take Yudhishthir up to heaven in his chariot. Indra suggested that they leave the dog behind, but Yudhishthir refused to go without the dog. It turned out that this was a test for Yudhishthir, and he had passed it. When he reached heaven, Yudhishthir was told that the Kauravs were in heaven as their sins had been forgiven, while his brothers and Draupadi were in hell. Yudhishthir insisted that he would stay in hell with his brothers and their wife. It was revealed that this was a test as well, the final one, which he had passed.

In more recent times, on 26 November 2008, armed terrorists of the Pakistan-based Lashkar-e-Taiba attacked Mumbai and killed 166 people, mostly civilians. The attack was widely reported all over the world.

I

HE EDITOR FELT at peace with himself. He stood at the top of Mount Meru with his hands on his hips. All around him there was the valley, and on the horizon, there were lesser peaks. Above him, the sky was an azure blue. He did not feel the cold of the snow on which he stood. Nor was he dazzled by its whiteness. The wind would have blown him away in his mortal life, but now he stood resolute, bare feet firm on the snow. He must be looking good in his dapper suit, he thought, a man of substance, standing tall at six-and-a-quarter feet, with his pony tail and his dark beard specked with gray. He could sense it: he had the look of a winner. He had lived his fifty-five years. He was a master of the universe.

The mongrel dog lay beside him, stretching lazily. Had he imagined it, or did the dog sometimes change expressions? Had a hint of pity entered the dog's gaze? He shrugged the thought off.

This was a time to reflect on grander things, a time to take note of his achievements. It had not been easy. He had played the role of... Chanakya, perhaps? Or Chanakya, Voltaire and Benjamin Franklin rolled into one person? It was a great responsibility: marshalling the thoughts of others, guiding them toward progress and true liberty, helping them shake off the shackles of a colonial past and reminding them that the choice between hope and despair was theirs. In his inexorable rise to become The Editor, he had had to make some compromises. He acknowledged that. All great statesmen compromised.

The biggest disappointment in his mortal life was missing out on the Padma Shri title. The paper had missed the informal revenue target that year, through no fault of his. But he had made sure the editor of *Hindustan's Voice* didn't get the title either. All that seemed so trivial now. He was here, at the pinnacle. There was no higher ground.

There had been six of them on the journey. The call girl, the terrorist, the driver, the constable, the politician and himself. And the seventh one, the dog—an unremarkable cur who had insisted on tagging along even though he had kicked it away at first.

In the beginning of their march up the icy slopes, the driver and the constable had tried to beat up the terrorist and realised it was no use. They had trudged in silence after that. He had wondered why they had been lumped together. Then, as the events unfolded, it all clicked. He himself was the common thread.

At the fag end of his mortal life, he had travelled to Mumbai and checked in at the Jat Hotel a night before his breakfast meeting with the politician, as he often did. In the morning, he called up the escort agency and described what he wanted. He had called his driver over to take the suitcase with the money to the safe house. The driver had a constable guarding him for safety. When the attack happened, he had been too dazed to think much.

Who could have imagined that all of them would be herded into the same room?

It was his room, and they were all in it, with the gun-toting terrorist. It had been nightmarish. He was ashamed that he had wetted his pants. 'Udha doon? Shall I blow them away?' the terrorist had asked, talking softly into his satellite phone, his eyes darting. He got his reply immediately. Then he ended the call. They all knew what would happen next, and it was a relief when it did.

Then they found themselves trudging up the icy slopes, avoiding each other's gazes most of the time. The terrorist had never looked up. He did not resist the blows of the driver and the constable and did not respond to their curses. He looked pensive and spent a lot of time staring at his palms. He stopped often to pray. The politician scowled most of the time. The call girl walked at a steady pace. She was completely expressionless. The driver and the constable walked together. The editor walked alone a little behind the group.

The brown dog was waiting for them as they turned a bend. It tagged along as if it was the most natural thing to do. The politician tried to shoo it away, but it just wagged its tail. At one point, The Editor was startled to find it just inches away from his trouser legs. He turned around and kicked it. The dog sat down and gave him a mournful gaze. The editor and the politician exchanged exasperated glances, and the Editor decided he would just let the cur be. They started to get used to its presence, and at a couple of forks it bounded ahead and showed them the easier path. After a while, they had allowed the dog to shepherd them.

The call girl was the first one to collapse into a heap. It was a bit strange. They rushed to her, and then realised that there was nothing to be done. She just lay there, quite still, without breathing. Without a word, they fell into line and pressed on. When the terrorist fell, The Editor realised what was happening. It was predictable after that. It was strange, this collapsing thing in their afterlives. The constable, the driver, the politician—they fell one by one, victims of their sins. And that left The Editor the last man standing. By then he had figured it out: he was Yudhishthir's heir. After that, he was nice to the dog. He even patted it a couple of times.

Now he stood in the snow, the dog at his feet, at the top, waiting for Indra's chariot. She appeared suddenly, standing a few feet away. The dog wagged his tail at the sight of her and bounded over to her. She crouched and hugged it, and whispered into its ear. It nodded and vanished. He looked around. There was no chariot.

He had never seen a woman so beautiful. She wore a white burkha with saffron and green markings. The green markings seemed to be in Urdu and the saffron ones were in Hindi or Sanskrit. They resembled lines from Sanskrit shlokas. Except for a few Oms, he couldn't read the script. Her hands were clasped, and her knuckles looked strained. She lowered her head and seemed to be in prayer. Apart from her hands, only her face was left uncovered by the burkha, and it was angelic. Of course, it would be. He wondered if it was true about paradise and the company of houris.

'Well, it's not true literally,' she said. 'First of all, a houri can be male as well.'

'I didn't mean, you know…' He was startled. 'So, you can figure out what I think, huh?'

She replied, 'Yes, we could converse without talking. But we'll talk so that it's easier for you.'

'By the way,' he said, 'about houris being male as well, I've always been an advocate of gay rights.'

She raised an eyebrow. 'Not always, perhaps?' She said. 'Anyway, I meant to offer an asexual perspective, not a homosexual one. But to really answer your question about houris, for those who talk about them, the idea is to convey a sense of bliss, I think. It's too bad they don't get to know the truth in their mortal lives.' He'd been trying to figure what was odd about her, and it struck him that she was completely still.

He smiled. 'I guess it'll take me a while to get the hang of things here,' he said. 'I was wondering why there's no, umm, you know, vehicle.'

'We won't need it,' she said gently. 'I think I need to explain this. You must be patient and you must introspect. Don't react immediately, okay?'
'Sure, okay.'

She seemed to need to make an effort to continue. Her fingers were still interlocked, and they trembled a bit. She said: 'It's like this: I sense that you correlated what just happened to you and your group with the story of Yudhishthir's final journey. That happens.'

He was puzzled. 'Do you mean it's not exactly true?'

'Unfortunately, it's exactly untrue—not Yudhishthir's story, but the correlation. What happened was that all of you, who were linked by a thread, were given an opportunity to reflect on your sins. As your fellow marchers realised their sins and repented, they were released from their transitory states.' She stopped. 'Am I making sense?'

'No, I don't quite get it,' he said a bit bluntly. He wasn't sure if he could tell her to cut the crap and get moving.

She smiled. 'Well, no, you can't, I'm afraid.'

'Oh, dear,' he said.

She laughed. 'But it's all right. I understand where you're coming from, as you people say. Now, let me try to make myself clearer, and do understand that I don't want to hurt you. I've been chosen for this discussion for a certain reason. I will see that the right thing is done.'

'You've been chosen? By whom?' he asked. 'Oh, of course. Stupid question.'

'Well, there are no stupid questions. The thing is, everyone in your group has gone in for judgement, roughly in decreasing order of their virtuousness during their earthly lives. We accept genuine repentance as a mitigating factor when slots are meted out. In your case, we waited for you to think, to introspect. Perhaps to ask forgiveness. But I understand that you were misled by the Yudhishthir story.'

He gaped. It took a while for him to react. Then he rasped, and his words rang shrill and loud. 'Are you—you can't tell me that they fell in the order of virtue! The call girl...' He stopped and sighed. 'Look, this must be a test. I really don't want to discuss this with you. Can I talk to your supervisor?' He found it hard to control his thoughts.

She looked down at her clasped hands. Her fingers were slender, and her nails trimmed short. When she spoke, her voice was steady. 'Even I don't talk to him very often, you know. Try to understand. You were given an opportunity to repent. I am here to talk to you, to encourage you to think about your mortal life, to awaken your conscience so that you use this opportunity to get a better slot than the one you are headed for.'

Something in her demeanour told him that there was no one else to talk to. 'I'm glad you understand that,' she continued.

He controlled himself. 'So, you're going to judge me, and you already have a view on my rating? Is this a fair trial?'

'I will judge you, yes, but you are not being tried. Remember, when we talk, the truth is known. You know it, and I know it. This is not like the courts down there, where the whole truth isn't always known, evidence isn't always available, and in our part of the mortal world, slightly more than in the richer parts, the judges can be bought.'

'If we know the truth, what's to discuss?' He ground his teeth. She held his stare and smiled.

'If you listen, if you think, if you are open, you may repent and there may be ways of atonement.'

'I still don't get it,' he shrugged. 'What did you mean by our part of the world? Are you Indian? Ex-Indian, I mean.'

She smiled. 'Roughly speaking, yes.'

'So how many of you handle the India cases?' 'It's only me.'

'Then you don't have too much time for me, I guess?' 'There is no time any more,' she said. 'Which means that there's plenty of time. About the judgement process,' she continued after a pause, 'the way I explain it is this: imagine you are between two mirrors. If you look straight and narrow at yourself, you will see yourself up close. If you look at anything else, you will see images reflected infinitely. That's how it is. I know everything about what you did. You should know by now that I know—and I know that you do, and it goes on. So do not think about the others. Do not deny your sins. Accept them, repent for them from the bottom of your heart and you will be better off.'

'That's interesting, but childish,' he said. He fingered the collar of his jacket. 'I've studied philosophy.'

She sighed. 'I haven't. I tried to explain it my way.'

'It's weird that you go on and on about my sins,' he said. 'Since you know, and I know you know and so on *ad infinitum*, do you mind telling me what I don't know: how the hell did I get ranked at the bottom of that group?'

'I wish you would look at yourself rather than the others. You know that it has already transpired. You cannot change that. Would you like to figure why you were ranked this way?'

He shrugged. 'I'm confused. I thought you said that there is no time any more. How come something's transpired?'

'There is no time,' she said, 'but there's still sequence. It's like a thread which was taut and has now become completely loose—only it doesn't go back to itself. But I sense that you find this childish. So, would you like me to explain the order to you, or would you like to try yourself? Remember introspection will lead to realisation.'

'You do it,' he thought.

II

She said: 'all right. But please understand I don't wish to hurt you. If you think I'm wrong, do correct me. First, about the call girl: she was forced into the trade. She was not the only one. Perhaps the media could bring the stories of those girls to light. But it wouldn't be convenient. She did sell herself, and she did sin. But she was a victim. We also look at how much hurt a person has caused. She hurt no one ever in her mortal life. She spent a lot of time in prayer, but we actually don't give points for that.'

'The terrorist was another victim. A murder cannot be pardoned, and he committed four. But he was born into a poor family in Pakistan, and he had three sisters. His father died young. You know what that means in there. He had two choices. The first choice was to convert from the Islam his father had taught him to the one which a new mullah taught. This would allow him to get enough money to give his family a life of ... no dishonour, let's put it that way. That money came from the US Treasury by the way, not the Pakistani treasury. It was from a small fund which is peanuts compared to the stimuli they'll be announcing soon. But I digress. The other choice was a nasty, short and brutish life.'

'Let me get this right, once again,' The editor interjected. 'You're saying that the call girl was the most virtuous, followed by the terrorist, and that I...' He didn't finish.

'It's not exactly that way,' she explained. She glanced at her clasped hands, sighed, and looked up again. 'They fell as soon as they truly repented for their sins. True repentance happens without fear of the punishment. It is self-contained; it arises from honestly engaging with your own soul. Still, it's true that the call girl was the most virtuous by our standards. As for the rest, there are some approximations which we need not go into.'

'But to continue: about the constable, it's funny, but he worked in a corrupt setup. We find these cases strange. You know, in departments like the civil construction department, they say that if you take bribes up to 2.5% of the contract value, you are honest. Anyone taking a higher cut is dishonest.' She shook her head and smiled.

The editor laughed. 'I didn't know that.'

'It's true,' she said. 'It's funny that the constable considered himself upright by the standards of his department, and it's sad that he was. He collected hafta from about a hundred people, including pimps, parking lot owners, stall owners and beggars. He bullied the meek and the oppressed from time to time, just for kicks, but not as often as he could have. On the other hand, he secretly saved many children, as many as he could, from the flesh trade. And when he had a choice between running away and facing the terrorists with his rusty rifle, he chose to fight.'

'Now, about the driver. There are millions like him. They are better off doing what they do than they would have been. This man worked up to sixteen hours a day. About the way he was treated— well, let me just say that you were not, umm, egalitarian. What he did do wrong was that he used to slip in a few fake notes into the suitcases every time he carried cash.'

'The bastard!' The editor shouted.

'Try not to curse. So you think he was unethical?' she smiled. 'Well, anyway, that and the fact that he was unfaithful to his wife, went against him. Also the fact that he wasn't, strictly speaking, forced into fraud. He was better off than his parents had been, he had a roof over his head and his wife worked as well. He was just easily tempted.'

'I treated him much better than a lot of others would have,' The editor said, in a softer tone. He was still shocked that the bastard was stealing his hard--earned money.

'I understand,' she said. 'As for the politician—well, what can I add? There's enough said about them.' She stopped, looked down at her open palms and looked into his eyes.

'And as for me?' He asked softly. 'I'm the prime accused in this trial, right?'

'Yes, of course, I was coming to you, and you're making me repeat this. You are not being tried. And let me tell you, I cannot lie. Of course, you only have my word for it.' She beamed.

He did not respond.

She went on. 'I don't mean to insult you, but if I have to summarise the situation I would do it this way: the politician clawed his way up to a life of luxury, and you were born into luxury. He was just about literate, while you were sent to the best universities in the world after you couldn't make it into the best institutes in India.'

'That's not true!' He interrupted. 'I wasn't interested anyway! In those institutes, I mean.'

'We shall let that pass. The point is that both of you took money which was … not rightly earned. But he took money for not doing his job—for bending the rules or breaking them. You, on the other hand, removed your old editor, took over the position, and used it to make money on the side for printing news. You created new rules. You had money flowing in any way, from advertisements. Like these full-page advertisements from the management guru.'

To his right, an image of his celebrated newspaper, *The Voice of India*, appeared. 'There are about a hundred business schools in the top ten in India, aren't there, if we believe all the ads in your paper?' She asked.

'How the hell did you do that?' He asked back.

'Try not to curse. How did I show you the newspaper?' She turned toward the display, shrugged and smiled.

'Yes. It's brilliant!'

'It's minor. Don't worry about the display technology. Do think about the issues.'

'About the B-school rankings,' he said. 'Are you blaming me for them? That's unfair! Have you ever seen a blurb exclaiming, "Latest #2 Bestseller?"'

She laughed. 'No, I haven't. You're right. Now let's focus on the issues. It's very important, and you will be better off forever if you do. You took money to print news, from those who wanted the news to be slanted in a certain way. With your synergy treaties, every square inch of the paper was on sale—not only the ad columns. You sold your soul.' The editor flinched. She pursed her lips. 'I'm sorry if I hurt you by saying that,' she said.

He inhaled deeply. 'You're right, this is not a trial. It's an inquisition. I refuse to defend myself. May I ask you some questions?'

There were furrows on her forehead. 'Of course, you may. But do remember what I told you. The whole truth isn't hidden. The evidence isn't needed. You are not being tried, and this is no inquisition. It's an opportunity we give to everyone, even the most immoral.'

'I'll ignore that last part,' he replied. 'Tell me, am I not a victim? Did I not have pressures from power centres?'

'Of course, you did, but the point is that you always had a choice. From the day you were born, you had enough money to last a lifetime. Your survival and basic dignity were never at stake. The stakes were lower, weren't they?'

He jabbed the air with his open right hand in the manner which he had developed. 'Lower? I guess you're being ironic. Tell me, why do we face these double standards? Isn't it true that the British magazine *The Wise Old Economist* justified the Iraq war? Wasn't that corrupt?'

'The thing is,' she said, 'you charted out a unique path in your mortal life. I could give you my views on someone else's sins. But first, I must try to make you see that you have sinned. Then, I must try to evoke repentance from you. Finally, I must assess the nature of your repentance and allot your slot for eternity. Those are the tasks at hand.' She looked down at her clasped hands. She frowned and seemed to make an effort to concentrate. When she looked up again, she spoke softly.

'Allow me to suggest something,' she said. 'Let's close our eyes. I will pray, and I request you to rethink everything.'

He looked into her dark brown eyes. 'Why don't you tell me what I should rethink,' he said, 'since you know more than I do about me.'

She intertwined her fingers and took a deep breath. 'Let me make it easier for you. Remember, please, that I'm trying to help you.' The editor raised his eyebrows, and she sighed.

'Look at this. The page next to your editorial page on 31 January 2007.' The display changed to a giant view of two pages of his newspaper. 'You published a story titled "Big breasted girls more prone to diabetes." It was based on a study conducted in *Toronto*, but that's beside the point. You've shown a pair of big breasts—for what? Clarity?' The editor exhaled loudly.

'Here's your cover story,' she continued, 'on 30 January 2008: "Monkey off Bhajji's Back." An Indian cricketer was charged with making a racist slur. You could have used the opportunity to examine if racism is a serious issue in India. Your paper just launched a jingoistic crusade.'

'Do you even know the background to all this?' The editor asked.

'Yes,' she said, nodding confidently. 'There's more: here's the cover story from 28 April 2008 about the mass outrage against the Bus Rapid Transit project in Delhi. All the well-meaning experts were trying to do was design a transport system for *people* instead of *cars*. Actually, the only outraged people were your readers—the affluent, whose cars hog the city's roads, and whose dignity is affronted by the sight of lesser people moving faster than them.'

The editor slumped and shook his head.

She joined her hands in a namaste, went on. 'Don't forget your messages to your new recruits: monetise, confectionalise, commoditise, fictiona-lise. The thing about paid news is that when you printed it, you ended up ignoring things that mattered, like hunger and deprivation. Or the arrest of a political prince at Boston airport, or the fact that this prince lied about his education. Who will stop this prince from becoming a king? And how will he do justice to more than a billion people?'

The editor raised his hand in a gesture to stop. 'What's the point of this discussion?' he asked. 'Is it to conclude that I never did a good thing in my life?'

'The heart of the matter,' she said, 'is simply that you had great power over the million most influential people. You did not use this power for the greater good of the one billion. What is worse, you exaggerated achievements, manipulated opinions and ignored real developmental issues. Together with the politician, you did more damage than thieves. When an average kind of thief—the type who gets convicted if he's caught—steals money, it's a zero-sum game for society. What someone loses, the thief gains. But when you took money, society lost a thousand rupees for every rupee you made.'

He gave her the look he reserved for such occasions. 'Is this some kind of moral science class? There's nothing new in these charges. They're frivolous. We also carried the *Bodhi Tree* column and serious economic columns. People see what they want to see. We were a pillar of democracy. We reflected the desires of our million readers. We were loyal to them. That's all there is to it.'

'I haven't finished,' she said. 'Look at the coverage of the Mumbai terror attacks.' She pointed toward the display, which now showed pictures of corpses. 'The paper and your website exponentially multiplied the terror. The website boasts that you got ten million hits during the time of the attacks. Your paper spread the message of terror, and multiplied the ineptitude of the government's response. Of course, you had been martyred by then.'

He stared at her. 'I wish you wouldn't give me these ones,' he said. 'Do you know how much money I gave to charity?'

'I don't think you've understood me. Or the gravity of the situation. We know how much money you gave to charity. We know it was less than one hundredth of a percent of what you made.'

'How the hell could you know that?' he said. 'It's a lie!'

She closed her eyes and contemplated her clasped hands. 'We know that you exploited journalists working under you in the name of mentoring them. I know that one of them... Do you remember a time when you called a journalist named Zubeida Shiekh to the Jat Hotel, and she called you up at the hotel to tell you that she wouldn't come?'

'I may have done what others would have liked to do. So, Dr Clinton is a philanthropist and I'm a philanderer?' He shot back.

'If you believe the media, people with a foundation named after them are philanthropists. If you ask us, only those are blessed who help others without boasting about it.'

He slumped and lowered his gaze and crossed his arms. Then the recognition dawned. There was a gleam in his eyes. 'It's you!'

'Yes, I was Zubeida in my mortal life. I quit the job and went back to Bihar. I spent the rest of my life there. It was shortened by the fact that I helped a hundred people out of poverty.' She looked at him and sighed.

'That's all it takes,' she continued. 'If the richest eleven million—the top one percent of society—each helped a hundred people out of poverty, things would be very different. But there's a combine at the top. That combine only deprives. Its greed knows no limits.'

'This is a farce!' The editor shouted. 'You have an axe to grind!'

He was blinded by her gaze. Then, he was blown off his feet by a gale. He fell on his back. The snow felt cold, and the brightness of the clear blue sky blinded him. When he got back on his feet, he was trembling. Everything seemed to have changed. She was twice as tall as him. The dog had reappeared. It was as high as his shoulders. It looked menacing.

Follow me, he thought he heard the dog say.

He turned to her, but she had turned her back to him. She knelt down and bent her head. He realised the meeting was over.

The dog started walking. It looked back and motioned The Editor to follow with a nod of its head. He knew that he did not have a choice.

III

SHE KNELT WITH her head bowed, her trembling hands in her lap. She felt the presence.

'You seem to be troubled,' the voice said.

'I am,' she replied. She made an effort to steady her hands. There was no reply.

'I am not sure about a few things,' she said. 'I felt anger when he said it wasn't fair, and I felt pride when I judged him as he should have been judged. Will you forgive me?'

The reply came: 'Can you think of the more relevant questions?'

'I will try.' She hesitated. 'Perhaps the question would be this: is it possible to separate pride from achievement, and anger from righteousness?'

'And what might be the answer?' The voice asked.

She thought about it. She looked up at the sky and took a deep breath of the icy air. 'They are not separable. But if the achievement and the righteousness are lasting, and the pride and the anger are fleeting, you might find them acceptable.'

'I suppose so,' the voice said. 'And what is the most important question?'

'That's easy,' she said. 'It is if I was correct in my judgement.'

'And why is it important?'

'Because I could have felt provoked to punish him more than he deserved, for trying to exploit me when I was young and vulnerable. Or I could have punished him less, to prove that I could forgive.'

'And is there not something that you wanted to discuss?'

She hesitated again. She traced the lines on her left palm with her right index finger. 'You know what it is, and I know you know ... but I feel ashamed.'

'And what does that mean?'

She lowered her head. 'It means that I am not yet one with you.'

'So, what do you conclude?'

She clasped her hands firmly. 'I have much more to look forward to,' she said.

'I am happy to hear that.' The voice, neither male nor female, was reassuring. 'If you say it now, you will be happy.'

The words came out quite simply. 'About that time, when The Editor had called me over, I was actually on my way to the hotel room. The bus broke down, and something snapped in me. I called him after that.'

'Was that difficult to admit?'

'Yes.'

'Do you feel better now?'

'I feel relieved.'

'Do you feel lesser now?'

She folded her arms and looked up. 'Not if you do not think me lesser.'

'And do you think I think you are lesser?'

'Nothing was hidden from you.'

'Then, coming back to the most important question: what is your answer?'

'Aham yathayogyam akarvam: I did as I should have done.'

'Does saying something in Sanskrit or Latin make it more profound?'

She thought for a while. 'Well, not by itself. I suppose if it's the same thing, then it doesn't become more profound.'

'Ah, I think you refer to ceteris paribus.'

She was puzzled, and then her face broke into creases and she burst out laughing. 'You're joking!'

'And I see that you are happy,' the voice said. She felt a caress, and then she knew she was alone.

She knelt in the snow with her hands in her lap. She felt at peace with herself.

Justice

DHRITARASHTR, BEING BLIND, had to concede the throne of Hastinapur to his younger half-brother, Pandu. Dhritarashtr's eldest son, Duryodhan, and Pandu's eldest son, Yudhishthir, were both contenders for the throne. At one point, Duryodhan visited the Pandavs' new palace. It was so shiny that he walked into a pool of water thinking it was a floor. Draupadi, the common wife of the Pandavs, taunted him for being a blind son of a blind father. Duryodhan took revenge later by humiliating Draupadi in his court after Yudhishthir lost her in a game of dice. Duryodhan slapped his thigh and asked Draupadi to sit on it. Bheem vowed to break Duryodhan's thigh.

The animosity between the Pandavs and Kauravs culminated in a great war. On the eighteenth day of battle, Duryodhan was one of the last men left standing among the Kauravs. Yudhishthir gave him the option of duelling with any one of the Pandavs with a weapon of his choice. He chose the strongest, Bheem, as his opponent and Bheem's favourite, the mace, as the weapon. Bheem defeated Duryodhan by hitting him on his thigh, against the martial code of conduct which prohibited hitting below the waist.

I

HEEM SMIRKED AS he taunted me. 'Are you blind?' He asked. His words always came out slow. He was the ugliest person I knew. He had sneered at me and my brothers so often and long that it had distorted his face permanently.

He looked down on me with that grin of his, which only made him uglier. My ribs still hurt from our fight in the orchard a few days ago. I could stand up to Bheem longer than anyone else, and I was working toward becoming a better wrestler than him when I turned sixteen, next year.

'Let me show you,' he said. He said each word like one of those moron monks reciting a verse. When the blow came, as usual, his hand moved like lightning. You would never expect it from someone so fat. He hit me a little to the left of my solar plexus so that I wouldn't get knocked out in one go. I fought back the tears. The water below us had a stench. It would have been a relief to fall off the tree trunk into the olid slush, but I would lose face. I focused my attention on a bird's cry, which sounded like it was saying, 'What did you do?' It helped me to ignore the pain. I had clenched my right fist and raised my left arm before he hit me. I was actually faster than him, but I had started too late. I put my weight behind the fist and, though I was out of breath, hit him back on the same spot. He was all muscle, and all slimy with sweat on that muggy day. My fist slid off his abdomen, and my knuckles hurt. It must have stung him, but he laughed.

'Bheem!' Two voices rang out. I looked behind. Yudhishthir was at the edge of the marsh. Even from a distance, I could see that he had put on his phoney pious look. A few yards behind him stood Guru Dron. 'Don't do that,' Yudhishthir commanded. He was always so keen to score points in the guru's presence.

'I was giving the blind man's son the big picture, ha ha,' Bheem laughed. The pain welled up in my chest, and my eyes watered. Bheem noticed that and his grin widened. I hated that feeling of weakness.

'Stop that!' Guru Dron's voice lashed out, and Bheem's expression and posture changed. His eyes dilated, and he grimaced and slouched. I looked into his eyes but did not laugh. I knew the guru was looking. 'Bheem, you know he climbed on to the trunk first. Step back and let him cross.'

Bheem turned without meeting my steady gaze and walked back toward his end of the trunk. I followed him. I stepped off the trunk and felt the cool mud form casts around my feet. It took an effort to pull my feet out at each step. I washed my sandals by shaking my feet one by one in the water when I reached the stony edge. I took my time so that I could speak without choking and my breath wouldn't appear ragged. I looked coolly at Yudhishthir and

Bheem, without saying a word, and greeted the guru with a namaste.

'Bheem, I am angry with you,' Guru Dron said. His forehead was wrinkled, but I noticed that the vein above his right eye did not throb. That meant he wasn't really angry. 'Tell me what you did wrong, please.'

'Guru-ji, I should have let him pass first.' Bheem hung his head, but anyone could see that he was faking contrition.

'No! That's not what I'm talking about!' Now the vein was throbbing. Sometimes he did try to be impartial—except when it came to Arjun.

'Be honest!' He was loud now. That was rare.

'Guru-ji, I should not have called him a blind man's son.'

'This is against Dharm! It's hitting below the waist!'

'I will not do it again,' Bheem mumbled.

'Talk loudly now!' The guru was still furious.

'I will never do it again.' Bheem looked at me. His eyes and mouth gave nothing away but his shoulders were tense.

'I believe you won't,' I said. I looked at Bheem, and then at Yudhishthir. I could never figure what went on in Yudhishthir's mind. I bent and did a namaste to the guru, and walked on.

I hated my father's blindness. For a while I even hated him. When you are small, your parents are like gods. You grow up a bit, and you start noticing their flaws. Then you only see the flaws. After you have grown up a bit more, you start to accept them with the flaws. All along, Father had known how I felt. I remembered the time, three new moons ago, when he had said to me: 'I know that I have not given you what other fathers give their sons. I wish you had a clear path to the throne. But this is how God made me.' He had put his hand around my shoulder, and he sounded all broken.

I felt his heart beating hard and fast while he looked expressionless. How often this must have happened. I felt a searing pain in my own chest. I said, 'I do not know anyone who has got more love from his father. The throne will be mine. And yours.'

I am ashamed to admit this: last winter, I shouted at Mother when she fell one more time. I ran into her chamber. She had a purple bruise on her forehead and was resting on a couch. I shouted: 'Why don't you take that blindfold off! Why should both my parents be cursed?' She had worn a blindfold since her marriage — after she got to know, too late, that Father was blind.

She was reaching out for me. She could recognise my footfalls. A smile had started to light up her face. Her hand paused. She quickly put on her mask and pulled her hand back. I was panting. I hated myself for wiping off that rare smile. I slowed down and walked to her. She placed four fingers on my cheek and then rested her palm there. 'Have I ever cried?' she asked. 'I who have much to cry about? And look at you, about to become a man soon.' I wiped my tears with her sari and sat with my head on her shoulder. I promised myself that would be the last time I cried. I couldn't have known better.

I walked on toward the gurukul, wondering what made me go across the tree trunk to the island in the corner of the lake. The workers used to go there sometimes to pick up vegetables. We—and the Pandavs—used it like a closed room, where no one could eavesdrop or see us. I had nothing much on my mind, nor had I needed to confer with my brother Dushasan. I realised that I was spending more and more time on my own, thinking about the past and the future, working scenarios out. I felt my biceps. They were taut and strong, but not good enough to beat Bheem.

'Guru-ji!' Bheem's voice was distant but it still boomed. I turned around. He was gesticulating wildly. He negotiated the span of the tree trunk in a few moments, with Yudhishthir behind him. Then they were panting and talking together to Guru Dron. The guru turned grave and beckoned me toward him.

II

WE ASSEMBLED IN the classroom—Guru Dron, Yudhishthir and I. 'I am unhappy about this,' the Guru said. He looked at Yudhishthir and at me in turn, with eyebrows raised. 'Valal has been murdered. The murderer has beheaded him quite neatly. No sword is missing from the armoury. It appears that only three persons have set foot on the island after Valal went there. Ahi, Daruk,' he looked at me, 'and you.'

'This is the second time I am seeing a murder in these parts. This time it's not inside the gurukul. But that won't console Valal's wife.' He stroked his chin and the strands of his gray beard swayed.

'I have duties toward gurukul employees. I become responsible for their lives and their acts when I take them into the establishment. Now, it is my duty to find out what happened and why, and to punish the one who committed the murder.' Out of the corner of my eye, I saw Yudhishthir run his fingers over his forehead. Someone must have told him that having a wide forehead was a sign of being intellectually gifted, and ever since, he had been fingering it, like a miser fool fondling his gold.

'As you are old enough now,' Guru Dron continued, 'and I do not want a kottapal interfering here, I ask you both: will you work together and solve the case for me?' As usual, I could not fathom what went on in Yudhishthir's complex mind. Before he could say anything, I said, 'Guru-ji, I am happy to work on this. But as you said, I have also been on the island after Valal went there. I know that I have committed no crime,' I trailed off.

'And I know it too,' the guru said. 'I asked Bheem and he said that he saw you going to the island, and you did not carry a sword. That gives me a little comfort. Don't forget that I will question you both on your findings. I will also want an account of every moment you spent on the island. I want to understand why Yudhishthir and Bheem saw the body and you did not.'

'Guru-ji,' I said, 'as for what I did, I really did nothing. I did not have a reason to go there, but I like the quiet there. I spent some moments there meditating and thinking. That is all I can say.' I shrugged. 'About why I did not see the body, it must be because I walked on the jungle path there to the other end of the island and came straight back. The body was definitely not anywhere close to my path. It must have been somewhere else.'

Guru Dron stroked his beard. 'That sounds about right. Yudhishthir, the body was in a clearing to the east?'

'That is correct, Guru-ji,' Yudhishthir thought for a while, frowned and nodded. 'Valal had gone to get mushrooms from there. A little later, Daruk and Ahi went together to plant seeds there.'

'What seeds?' The guru asked. 'How much later?'

Yudhishthir hesitated. 'I haven't spoken to them, Sir. This is what I heard.'

The guru leaned his head to his right and narrowed his eyes. 'You both will report to me before dusk today. And I do not want to hear anything vague then.' He looked at Yudhishthir first, and then at me, and flicked an index finger. 'Go now.'

We hastily bowed and stepped out. I had a mild heady feeling. This was the closest I had seen Yudhishthir come to getting scolded by Guru Dron in a long time.

'Do you have a plan for the investigation?' Yudhishthir asked me. His words came out a bit meek.

'No,' I replied. 'Do you?'

'Yes.' He sounded more confident now. 'I thought we should talk to Ahi and Daruk, separately and together, and figure out which of them is the killer.'

'Sounds like a plan, but are you sure it's one of them?'

Yudhishthir looked surprised. 'No, but who else can you think of, under the circumstances?'

'No one,' I shrugged.

He folded his arms and gave me that superior look.

'I was thinking that in terms of opportunity, there's just the three of us—Ahi, Daruk and … me.' I said. 'But maybe if we look at motive, there may be someone else.' I enjoyed the way his eyebrows went up. 'Anyway,' I continued, 'as you say, we have to talk to those two first.'

III

WE HAD ASKED Daruk to wait outside. Ahi's lips quavered. He had innocence written all over his face, I thought. The air was muggy, and there were beads of sweat on his lined forehead. He stood hunched, with his fingers clamped tightly. I would have put his age at more than thirty. His breath came out noisy, giving away his nervousness.

Yudhishthir exuded nobility—or so he thought. He was just a bit taller than me, and he looked down on the squat servant. 'So,' he said, 'tell us, there are five of you here?' The way he talked, you would think he was dropping pearls of wisdom if he told you that he would be back after taking a leak.

'Yes, Prince.' We could hardly hear him.

'Speak up!' Yudhishthir was loud and even I was startled. 'What do you do? Tell us how you all are organised.' I already knew all about that, but I stayed quiet.

Ahi cleared his throat. 'Well, Sir, Daruk and I perform farming duties and take care of the animals. I came in place of a man named Ugna, as you might know. The guru likes to work the farms himself, and you Sirs also, of course. But we do the regular work. Valal was the gardener, he would also work with us sometimes. Then there is Ballav, the lame one, who cooks. And Tantipal, who acts as a messenger most of the time, but he is also a carpenter when he is here...' Yudhishthir raised an arm to stop him, and Ahi gulped.

'Did you say carpenter?' Yudhishthir asked. He seemed excited. 'When did he go? And where?'

I had been eyeing a buzzing fly on the wooden pillar next to us for some time. It became still for an instant, and I swatted it with my palm. Ahi cringed at the smack, and Yudhishthir frowned. I enjoyed the moment but kept a straight face.

'Sir,' Ahi continued after Yudhishthir motioned him, 'he left four days ago. He said that he was headed for Mithila, and would return in many new moons. Guru-ji will know more about that.'

'Hmm.' Yudhishthir ran a thumb across his furrowed forehead. He turned his head and looked at me, and I nodded to acknowledge his look. 'Now, tell us, moment by moment, what you and Daruk did today. Start at the beginning. Do not leave out any detail!'

Ahi started his story. Early in the morning, Kripi mata gave orders to Ballav, the cook, for the day. Then, Ballav asked Valal to get mushrooms from the island. Valal used to poke Ballav very often for being lame, but on that day he didn't. He set off toward the island when the shadows were still long. Ahi saw Valal walk past him and Daruk while they were working the paddy field. Daruk called out to Valal and asked him to wait for them, as they were about to go to the island next, but Valal said he was in a hurry and had much more work lined up for the day. Ahi and Daruk followed Valal to the island, but they were not surprised when they did not see him. The mushroom farm that he had gone to was on the other side of the island, the eastern side. Anyway, Valal might have returned with the mushrooms and given them to Ballav. They came back over the tree trunk just before I did. Kripi mata had seen them going to the island carrying only a pouch of seeds and their spades, and they had greeted her. I clearly remembered that they only carried a small spade each, and I mentioned this to Yudhishthir.

Ahi started to slink away after giving us his story. 'Wait!' Yudhishthir commanded. 'What seeds did you plant?'

'Carrot and gourd, Sir.'

'What did Valal poke Ballav about?' Yudhishthir asked.

I felt a pang of guilt. I had gone to the kitchen once, to convey a message from Kripi mata, and walked in on Ahi and Daruk joking about how they should get Ballav to hobble about in the paddy field, about how it would help to mix up the soil. Instead of scolding them, I had smiled at the idea.

Ahi hesitated. 'Well, you know he is lame. Guru-ji adopted him, and...'

'And what?' Yudhishthir asked.

'His wife is blind.' Ahi gulped. He turned his eyes away from me. I did not react.

'And Ballav is only lame, right?'

'Yes, Sir. He only gets duties which do not require him to move around too much. One of his legs is shorter than the other.'

'Who went to the island yesterday?' I asked my first question.

Ahi thought a bit. 'Daruk went to take a look at the place, and to clear it a bit, while I worked here.'

'What did he clear it with?' I asked.

Ahi's eyes widened. 'Sir, with a scythe, the blunt scythes we use. They are very blunt...' He trailed off.

'Wait outside,' Yudhishthir said, 'and send Daruk in.'

Daruk's story tallied with Ahi's. The scythe he had used was in the hut where they stored implements. We called them in together. It was the same. There were no cracks in the story.

Earlier we had seen the corpse before it was taken away for cremation. It was a horrible sight for me back then, before all the blood flowed in the war. His widow's wails travelled the long distance from their cluster of huts in the north-east corner of the gurukul. It was a relief that she would be taken care of by Guru-ji and Kripi mata.

We dismissed Ahi and Daruk after some more pointless questioning which Yudhishthir subjected them to. I didn't waste my breath on it.

There was this idea shaping up in my mind. 'Yudhishthir,' I said, 'do you know what's the key to this case?'

'Of course, the sword. Where is it? Or is it some other weapon?'

He was sharp, I had to grant him that. Not as much as he appeared to be, not enough to deserve the fawning of Guru-ji. But he was sharp all right.

'And where can it be?' I asked. 'In the lake, of course!'

'And what's the fastest way of getting it?'

'Well, we can call our brothers.' He hesitated a bit. 'It'll be smoother if you let us Kauravs do this, perhaps?' I said. 'There are more of us and there will be less friction, no?'

Yudhishthir frowned, thought a bit and nodded. It would be faster and smoother this way.

IV

I LAY SPENT, on my belly, with my chin resting on my fingers, on the grassy shore of the lake. Its waters had turned frothy from the strokes of my brothers, but there was no sign of the sword. The film of sweat and water on my back refused to dry up in that oppressive, dank air. My hair was still matted. My brothers' strokes and their yells drowned out the never-ending bird song which I was fond of listening to. I loved the fresh smell of the grass. The water was brown close by, green at the far edge and countless shades in between. I thought of Father not being able to see, and Mother wearing her blindfold in her pointless protest against being tricked into the marriage. I realised I had clenched my fists and relaxed them with an effort.

My view was blocked by one of my brothers, panting as he ran toward me with the unsteady steps of one who has been swimming for a long time. 'Brother, what now? Should we give up?' He asked me.

I flexed my arm muscles and looked up at him. He flinched.

'Well, tell us.'

'Spend another couple of hours and search every part of it! No wait, I'll join in again!'

The water was hot. It wasn't long before I sensed a commotion not too far away. Two of them were fighting over a sword. I got there, gave them a club each, and made them point out exactly where it had been. It had been lying flat on the bed of the lake, a few feet away from the far shore, at the point where it was farthest from the island.

I swam with it for a while and then started to plod on the bed of the lake. My brothers crowded around me as I examined it. It was not one of ours. It was more like the ones the Nishads of the jungle used. The blade was shorter so that it was more useful at close quarters. The hilt was plain, as their men did not have much use for adornment, unlike us.

I told my brother Dushasan to take the sword to Yudhishthir and ask him to wait for me. I dispatched the rest of my brothers and walked toward the gurukul. On an impulse, I walked straight to the north-east cluster where the servants lived. I waited under the pipal tree for a while. I thought of the cleanliness with which sacrifices were performed in the gurukul. Some things were clear, some weren't. I remembered the time when Ahi and Daruk had been teasing Ballav. About my giving weight to it when I smiled. That was shameful.

I walked on toward the servants' huts, with an idea in my mind. I wanted to confirm that there was a wet loincloth drying in front of one of the huts, as I expected. But then it struck me that it need not have been left to dry outside. And it need not have been left to dry at all. With the sword at the bottom of the lake and no witnesses, there was no evidence. The loincloth would dry anyway, like mine was drying while I wore it.

I turned back toward the hut where Yudhishthir was waiting for me. He was examining the sword with the practised eye of the keenest of connoisseurs.

'This is not one of ours. The Nishads use these,' he pronounced. His lips were pursed, and he exuded concentration and intellect. I stayed quiet.

'You can make out from the length, and—'

'The hilt,' I finished for him.

'Yes,' he said. 'So, what does that mean?'

'What?' I asked him. I should have stayed out for a while, focusing my thoughts. There were memories, some of them blurred. I remembered my gaze lingering, a little longer than it should have, on Ballav's wife. I had cursed myself for salivating at her blindness, for even thinking about a married woman.

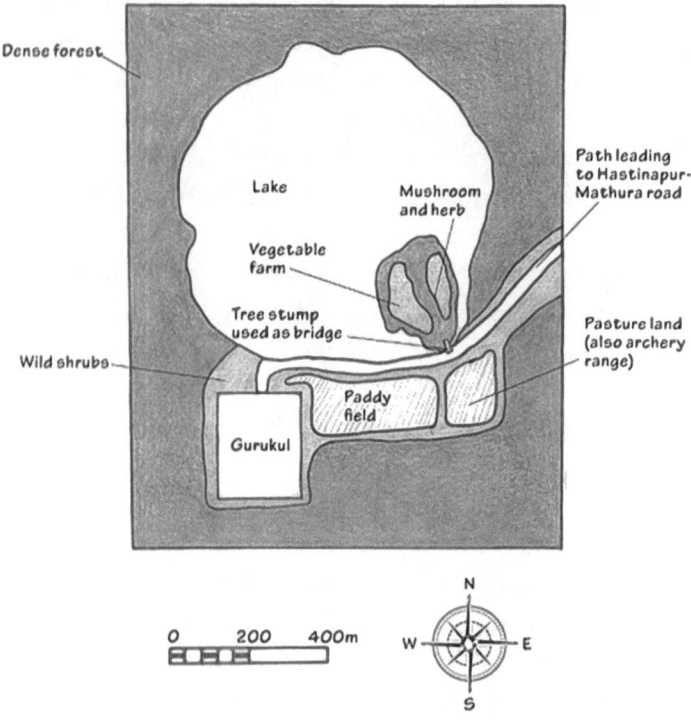

Rough sketch of the Gurukul's vicinity,
including the island in the lake

What were the chances that she had not figured in the jibes directed at Ballav?

I thought of his bulging muscles, unusual for a cook but natural for someone who had to perform so many gurukul duties.

What and how—I thought I knew almost for certain the answers to these questions. Why? That was always the more important question. And I was beginning to understand.

I had missed out most of what Yudhishthir said. 'On the other hand,' he continued, 'one has to be very strong to skilfully use it. Do you agree?'

'Yes, more or less,' I said.

'Less of what?'

I wiped the sweat trickling down over my eyebrows with my hand. 'Well,' I said, 'I was thinking about why? We have to be clear about that.'

'You're right. We haven't had any trouble with them since the time with Eklavya.' He faltered a bit at the name. 'But then there's been a bit of a dispute about clearing the jungle, and especially about the island. Should that have led to a murder? I don't think so. But what else can it be?'

I looked at him. 'True. Nothing else.'

V

WE WERE IN our classroom again. Guru-ji sat on the platform, exuding calm, while we stood facing him.

When he stood in front of us a few seasons ago, he looked down to talk to us. Now he looked straight at us when he stood. Our world was changing. I sensed that command over others would come more easily to the one who assumed a right to command them. And to command others, you must detach your outer and inner self. Guru-ji was a master at it, and so was Yudhishthir. But I could learn, and this would be good practice.

'Have you come with a complete report?' he asked. We looked at each other, and I nodded to Yudhishthir to signal that he could take the lead. 'Yes, Guru-ji,' he said.

'Tell me.'

'Guru-ji,' Yudhishthir began in an earnest manner, 'we first talked to Ahi and Daruk separately. That helped us to establish that they did not carry any weapon on to the island.'

'Impossible,' Guru-ji said. 'Sir?'

'That cannot be. Talking to them could not have established that they did not carry any weapon to the island.'

'Sir, yes Sir, what I meant—,' Yudhishthir stammered and I kept a straight face.

'Is that you tallied their versions with each other, and with the fact that they took Kripi's name, which you assumed they would not do lightly, and therefore you left this statement unverified.' Guru Dron's words were soft and menacing. 'This is not what I expect from you, princes,' he said.

And what would he know about princely behaviour, I thought. He stared at me almost as if he had heard me. I had to lower my gaze. A peacock's cries broke the uncomfortable silence.

Yudhishthir gulped and continued. Guru Dron interrupted him several times. By the time Yudhishthir was done, he had beads of sweat on his forehead. I realised that my forehead was damp too. Guru Dron was quiet for a while, and he traced one strand of his beard with the nail of his little finger. Then he rotated his head, in the manner he adopted when he was lost in thought.

'You,' he pointed at me. My heart pounded a bit. But it wasn't like the old days, when he was like a god to me. Shakuni Mama had helped me make myself mentally stronger. 'You haven't talked. What do you have to say about all this?'

'Guru-ji,' I replied, 'we have worked together, as you ordered. As Yudhishthir explained, all indications are that the murder must be the work of the Nishads. First of all, they have a problem with our using the island for our needs. Second, all of us who were there on the spot, including me, of course, did not have a strong enough motive to kill Valal. More importantly, we did not have a weapon, unless it was concealed earlier by one of us. Finally, the type of weapon points to the killer being a Nishad. On the other hand, he could also be someone who cleverly used a sword obtained from the Nishads, but that seems very unlikely.'

'So,' Guru Dron said as he continued to play with his beard, 'a Nishad swam across the lake, committed the act... I agree that is most likely. But do you know what the problem with your solution is?'

'Yes, Guru-ji,' I said. 'Why did the Nishad leave the sword behind? And why did he leave it at that spot? In fact, when Yudhishthir and I first thought of searching the lake we imagined someone throwing the sword into the lake from the island. At that point, we still figured that the killer used the tree trunk to get onto the island and come back.'

'You're right.' Guru Dron didn't look happy, but I sensed he was pleased with my analysis. 'And I think the answer is that the killer didn't want someone on the shore to see the sword in his hands or tied to his back. Yes. It would be most unusual. He may have thought he would come back and get it later.'

He rotated his head again once, and then clasped his hands behind his neck. 'What intrigues me is that this is the second time I'm faced with a murder here, and we're pointing to the Nishads. Are we creating a bogey?'

He was quiet for a while. We knew we weren't expected to answer.

'But what else could it be? The sword, the motive, the timing.' He stood up in a fluid movement, without using his hands to support himself. 'And I need to think about how we must respond. We can go to war and crush them, but I don't think we will do that.'

'Guru-ji, may I suggest something?' I asked. Yudhishthir's eyes widened.

'Yes.'

'Guru-ji, Ballav is the one here who has contact with the Nishads. He buys rare herbs from them. I think I can go and talk to him, so that he tells them that we suspect them, and we will hit them hard if they provoke us again.'

The guru nodded. 'Good idea. That is not the way to deliver the message, though. Ballav should tell them to convey the message to the local chief that I, Dron, the Royal Tutor, have taken note that the murder weapon used belonged to them. That is all he should say, in exactly those words. Nothing else. Is that clear?'

'Yes, Guru-ji.'

'That should end the matter. You may go now.'

Once we were outside, I said goodbye to Yudhishthir. He looked a bit surprised, but I explained to him that it was better for me to talk to Ballav alone. It was a simple task, and I knew him from his stint as cook in the Hastinapur palace.

VI

THE SUN HAD mellowed a bit, and the shadows were lengthening, but my throat was parched. The humid heat was like an endless, invisible sheet of silk which I walked against. I realised I had not drunk water since we got started on the investigation. The smell of medicine wafted out of the kitchen, suppressing the more pleasant scent of the jungle. The shrill hum of the insects was louder, or perhaps I imagined it that way.

I was tired, and I would be glad to see the end of this long day. But it was a day which had given me a sense of accomplishment. My thoughts had become clearer. I stroked my right arm and felt the comforting curve of my biceps. My sandals rang loud and clear on the caked mud of the approach to the doorway.

Ballav stood there, stirring a brownish liquid in a large brass pot. The bubbling of liquid was the loudest sound in the hall. He bowed a bit jerkily and then looked up at me, even as his hands continued their circulatory motion. I sensed the irregular rise and fall of his chest as he tried to control his breath. I nodded to acknowledge his bow but stayed quiet. It was cooler inside, but his forehead and shoulders turned shiny with sweat. I stretched upwards and interlocked my arms, feeling my muscles with my fingers. Then I looked straight toward his eyes. He did not meet my gaze.

He slumped, made an effort to straighten up and looked at me. 'What is it, Prince?' He had to clear his throat before the words would come out.

'I have a feeling you swim very well,' I said.

His eyes were downcast again, and he was quiet. He let go of the stick, hobbled toward me and went down on his knees. He was shivering. It was a while before he looked at me.

'Prince, you cannot imagine …,' he searched for words.

'How much they tormented you?' I said.

He nodded. 'And for so many years!' His lips trembled.

His arms were brutishly strong, I noticed, and he had pleasing looks. If it hadn't been for that one deformity. I realised that even if I had wanted to, I would not have had it in me to convict this man.

'So, you think it was all right to take his life?' I asked. I kept my voice low, knowing it would sound menacing.

He took a few breaths before replying. 'There was no choice!' His words came out very loud, and he looked startled himself. He lowered his voice. 'Prince, they made fun of me all the time, but they should not have come close to my honour. There is a line, a lakshman rekha!' He shook his head and stood up without taking the support of his hands. He was calm now. He folded his hands in a salute, and said, 'I salute you, Prince, for having figured it out. I will take the punishment.'

'I have not completely figured it out,' I said. 'How, I know. You expected us to think of the island as a closed area, with the only access being the log. You were the only one who could have got the sword from the Nishads. It actually didn't make sense for a Nishad to drop the sword at the edge of the lake, but for you the lake was the obvious place to throw it. You had the ability to detach a head cleanly. But why exactly? Did you kill him so that Ahi and Daruk would be implicated?'

He nodded.

'You supposed we would not suspect you? We would not imagine you moving fast enough?'

He lowered his head.

'Don't you have anything to say?'

He looked up at me. His face was still long, but his gaze was steady. 'I will not ask for mercy, Prince,' he gulped. 'I did right. I will sleep in peace tonight.'

I thought that over as I focused on the spot between my eyebrows with my eyes closed. I felt as if a burden had been lifted from me. I could not have put it in words, but I knew I had found a direction. It became clear that the right thing to do was to follow my heart. To strengthen my arms so they could follow it. To gather others behind me if more arms were needed. Not to calculate the consequences. Not to forget an insult.

It must have taken me some time. I sensed Ballav standing up in a jerky movement, pushing himself up with his hands. He stood bent, with his palms joined. He was looking at me, waiting for me to speak.

I quickly told him about the message to the Nishads, so that he would know. He looked puzzled. I said, 'And remember I spared you.' I turned around quickly, but not before I saw his eyes widen and his shoulders sag with relief.

'Prince! Suyodhan!' he called out. 'I will remember this.'

I turned my head a bit, not all the way. 'I will be called Duryodhan,' I said. I walked on.

The Examination

At one point in the *Mahabharat,* during the Pandavs's exile in the jungle, they were thirsty, and Nakul went to fetch water for all of them. He found a lake, but when he was about to drink its water, the spirit of the lake stopped him and told him he would die if he drank the water without answering the spirit's questions. Nakul ignored the warning, drank the water, and became lifeless. Sahdev, Arjun and Bheem followed Nakul one by one, and went through the same fate. The virtuous Yudhishthir followed his brothers, but he heeded the spirit's warning and brought his brothers back to life by answering a series of questions put to him by the spirit guarding a lake. Yudhishthir's answers to the questions provide insight into Hindu values.

In the original text (as translated by C. R. Rajagopalachari), for example, the spirit asked, 'What is that which, by giving up, man becomes rich?,' and Yudhishthir replied: 'Desire. Getting rid of it, man becomes wealthy.' The spirit asked: 'What is the greatest wonder in the world?' Yudhishthir replied: 'Every day, men see creatures depart this world and yet, those who remain seek to live forever.'

In this story the questions are unchanged, but the answers reflect modern times.

I

 HARAM RAJ FELT better. A numbness had set into his clenched pelvis and it soothed the rest of him. He often marvelled at the varied colours of nipples of Indian women. To him, they were the true embodiment of unity in diversity. He wondered what the angel's nipples looked like. It wasn't his fault the thought came to his mind: he tried to guess what they would be like, and the silvery atmosphere tended to suppress colour.

Her gaze turned colder, and she frowned without losing her serenity. 'I would think about more important points if I were you,' she said.

'I'm sorry,' Dharam Raj said. He really was. With his four dead colleagues strewn around him in rather undignified positions, with their trousers unzipped, with his bladder about to burst, in this strange dreamy situation, he really should focus on the task at hand.

The five of them had been drinking together since sundown, in the state guesthouse by the lake in the middle of the Rampur forest range. They had gone there as part of their enquiry into deer poaching.

Dharam Raj was already looking forward to the day, five years from now, when the results of the fast-track enquiry would be out. He was sure the seminal Dharam Raj Committee report would be widely cited. He could kick-start the citations.

He had lost count of how many Black Label and soda pegs he'd had by the time he stepped out of the main hall and walked toward the lake with fast but doddering steps. The Black Label had done its job, as always. He couldn't be higher than he was. He had helped himself to another one while he waited for the others to return. Nakul Chandra was the one who came up with the idea of walking over to the lake and peeing into it. He had announced what he was going to do as he stood swaying, glass in one hand and cigarette in the other. Sachdev Kumar said he would join in. A little later, Bheem Singh said he needed to pee and would check what the others were up to. Then, Arjun Tripathi said he might as well lighten himself with the others. Dharam Raj had just started to sip a peg, and he decided to hold on for some more time.

A little later, he had downed the peg and none of them had come back. The waiter had also left after pouring the last round of drinks. When he reflected on it later, Dharam Raj thought that maybe he should have been scared then. But he wasn't. He walked out into the cool full moon night. As he got closer to the lake and saw the huddled shapes, he first thought he should run back and get help, but something propelled him forward. His thoughts were muddled—he was thinking that he must pee, he must not wet his pants, he must get help… He forced himself to calm down by focusing on his pounding heart. It had been a long time since he had needed to do that. Usually he was the one making others' hearts pound.

Sachdev was the only man lying on his belly. Dharam Raj turned him over. He looked around carefully. They were all sprawled by the side of the lake, all four of them, with their flies open. Arjun Tripathi's shrivelled member drooped out. What an ugly sight it was. To a man, nothing was uglier than another's organ. He couldn't help noting that his was probably bigger than Arjun's. That was better, he thought, he was getting a grip on himself. He noted that there were no signs of struggle. Their faces weren't contorted. In fact, they were completely at peace. It was weird. He would not have believed it if it had not been right in front of him.

He took a few deep breaths and took in the scent of the jungle and the lake, a blend of a million individual scents. He noticed that it was not a silent night at all—there was a high-pitched, soft, throbbing drone which he hadn't noticed till then. The moonlight was bright enough for him to make out the features of each of the faces. He thought he must be imagining it, but the scent turned a little stronger, the noise a little louder and the light a little brighter.

Was the place haunted? He had never believed in ghost stories, but he couldn't help getting the feeling that he was in one. His four friends did look like a spirit had knocked them out. He shivered and shook his head. He must get in control.

First of all, he thought, he must pee, and then go back for help. He hadn't carried his mobile here. Of course. He was surprised that the urge to pee had actually become less intense. But it was still there. He unzipped himself.

'Don't do that, please,' a voice boomed. A woman's voice, soft but firm. Was he going nuts? Was it the liquor?

She appeared suddenly. She stood a few feet away. On the water! He had never seen a woman so beautiful. She wore a white burkha with coloured markings which seemed to be in Arabic and in Sanskrit. Her hands were clasped. Apart from her hands, only her face was left uncovered by the burkha, and it was angelic.

It must be the liquor, he thought. 'Why do you think so?' she asked.

'How can this be?' he mumbled.

'Does that matter? Isn't it enough that it is happening?' She smiled.

He stood silently. His breathing had turned ragged. He pushed a nail into his left arm and ran it till his wrist. It hurt. So, it was happening.

'Yes, it is happening,' she said. 'If you can see, hear, smell and feel it, that's enough evidence for you to judge if it's happening. You are the witness yourself.'

Yes, he thought, this is happening. What is this?

'This is a short cross-examination. Don't look so startled. We can converse without your talking, okay?'

He took this in. It took a while. Then he nodded. 'Yes,' he said.

'Now, it's all very simple. You see, each of these four didn't stop when I asked them to, and you see what happened to them. I see you are wiser. You did heed me.'

Dharam Raj realised that he still had his fly open. He zipped it up. The pressure was just short of unbearable. 'What is all this? Who are you?'

'Well, the first and the important thing is that you must not urinate now. Answer my questions, and I might set all of you free. But if you get a single question wrong, you will join your colleagues here. Do you believe me?' She stood there, on the water, looking down at her clasped hands, and then straight into his eyes.

'Yes,' he said. He realised he was slouching. He drew himself up and spoke a bit louder. 'Please, what is this about? Is it too much to ask?'

'No. But it might be too much for your bladder to bear. So why don't you let me start the questions?'

He had been wondering what was different. Now he got it. It was silvery all over. There were many shades of black and white, but there was no colour. His mind wandered to her nipples. That was when she scolded him.

'Can we start with the questions now?' She asked.

'Yes,' he said.

II

'WHAT MAKES THE sun shine every day?'

He thought very hard. What was it? 'First, I have to ask you, do I tell you what should be, or what is?'

'What is. It's in the question. And let me make it easier for you—don't bother to say it. Just think it. Anyway, you can't hide what you're thinking from me. How does that sound?'

Okay, he thought.

'So, what makes the sun shine every day?'

His mind went blank. He took a few deep breaths.

The Gandhi family? he thought.

'Correct. What rescues man in danger?'

A phone call to the SHO.

'Yes, but tell me, and this is not in the list of questions, why are you sweating? Try to relax a bit.' She smiled. She had dimples.

Dharam Raj realised he was clammy all over, in that cool air. It's strange, he thought, he was actually known to be very calm in conflict situations.

'I believe so. Let's continue. By the study of which science does a man become wise?'

A man becomes wise by learning how to bribe, not by studying any science.

'What is more nobly sustaining than the earth?'

A Swiss bank account.

'What is higher than the sky?'

A pile of the files of pending court cases.

'What is more fleeting than wind?'

News on the asking rates for judicial services.

'What is more blighted than a withered straw?'

A judge who can't find a reason to adjourn a hearing.

'What befriends a traveller?'

An escort service.

'Who is the friend of the one who stays at home?'

Paid news channels.

'Who accompanies a man in death?'

He goes alone, accompanied by body hair where he doesn't want it.

'Which is the biggest vessel?'

A politician's belly.

'What is happiness?'

A rival getting a bad annual rating.

'What is that, abandoning which, man will be loved by all?'

Reluctance to take bribes.

'What is the loss which yields joy instead of sorrow?'

Loss of semen.

'What is that which, by giving up, man becomes rich?'

Reluctance to give bribes.

'What makes one a real Brahman? Is it birth, good conduct or learning?'

None of them. A backward caste certificate issued by me.

'What is the greatest wonder in the world?'

Everyone here thinks everyone else is more corrupt than him.

'Or her. Well, what can I say? Except congratulations. You've mostly done fairly well.'

Dharam Raj was tired. He thought, *what now? Will I be showered with flower petals from the sky?*

She smiled, and he noticed the dimples again. He felt a splotch on his right shoulder. It was a bird dropping. It wasn't too smelly—as he often commented in private, there's no shit as odious as human shit—but it broke his spirit. 'No! No! No!' He shouted. 'This is …,' he stopped. 'Please, please let me go,' he mumbled.

'Sure,' she said, 'but why don't you choose one of your friends for me to revive?'

'Why one?' He asked. 'Why not?'

He felt his jowls on his chest and realised he was slumping. This had to end soon. *Okay,* he thought, *I choose Nakul Chandra.*

The angel folded her hands. 'And why did you make that choice?'

You already know that. He owes me money.

'You've been very honest,' she said. 'I'm pleased. I'll grant them all their lives.' She vanished, just like that. There weren't even ripples on the lake.

He knelt first, and then crashed on the ground. The grass was dewy and soft.

III

HE CLOSED HIS eyes only for a moment and when he opened them again the four of his friends had surrounded him. They looked very serious. He thought they would have been smiling and grateful, but they seemed to be angry about something. Nakul and Arjun started to shake him.

'Let me be. I'm tired,' he shouted.

'Did you hear that? He's tired, he says!' It was Bheem Singh's voice.

Dharam Raj's throat was parched, his head hurt like hell and the light blinded him. When he got used to it, he recognised a peculiar face-shaped mark on the wall plaster and realised he was in his bed in the guesthouse, and the four of them had crowded into his room. Their laughter was raucous.

'He's up now!' Bheem shouted. There was a bit of backslapping. Their faces came into focus slowly.

Dharam Raj bolted up and then walked to the sink in the corner. He realised he was limping. His knees hurt like hell. He splashed water onto his eyes. One of the men handed him a bottle of water, and he gulped from it greedily and then put it on the sink. He stood with his back leaning on the wall. He realised he was wearing his crumpled trousers.

'What's up?' His voice was a croak. He cleared his throat.

'What's up, he asks!' It was Sachdev Kumar this time. The merriment continued. Sachdev walked up and bounced Dharam Raj's belly up and down, holding it from below. 'Ha ha,' he said. 'What's up is that we had to lift you up from the lake shore and carry you here, you rascal!'

'You bunch of… I actually saved your lives!' He was still a bit hoarse.

This time the laughter was louder. 'Saved our lives, oh man. This is priceless!' Arjun was holding on to his stomach.

'You ungrateful bastards,' Dharam Raj was louder. 'I actually faced those questions!' Their looks made him hesitate. 'From the angel,' he said. They laughed even harder. He knew he should stop then. The light was so bright that it almost hurt. Dharam Raj drew himself to his full height and said, 'Okay, that's enough. I'll come down in a while for breakfast.'

Arjun crashed into the bed and Sachdev was wiping his eyes. The other two were getting hysterical.

Sachdev said, 'Dharam Raj-ji, it's time for lunch. It's 12.30.'

After some time and much persuasion, Dharam Raj got them to leave him alone. He told them he would join them in half an hour after freshening up. They were still repeating his words to each other while they walked out. He knew he had given them enough material to rag him for the rest of his life. With his head in his hands, he sat there for a while, wondering about it all. It must have been a dream. He must get over it. He needed to propel himself with his hands when he got up.

As he got up, he noticed the scratch he'd made with his nail on his left arm. Then he saw his shirt placed neatly on the backrest of a chair. It still had the splotch of bird shit on the shoulder.

HONOUR

BEFORE SHE WAS married, a sage gave Kunti a boon by which she could call on any god and get a child from him. Kunti was impetuous and she called on the Sun god to see if the boon worked. She was blessed with a boy, Karn, but she had to abandon him because she was unwed. She set him afloat on a river, in a basket. The baby was adopted by Adhirata, who was King Dhritarashtr's charioteer. Karn grew up to become a great warrior. He challenged Arjun, the best warrior among the Pandavs, to a duel in a public tournament. The royal guru, Kripa, refused to allow the duel, saying that only equals could engage in love and battle. In order to make him eligible to duel Arjun, Duryodhan pronounced Karn King of Anga on the spot. Karn asked how he could repay Duryodhan. Duryodhan said that he wanted Karn's friendship.

Before the great war, Krishna and Kunti approached Karn separately and asked him to join the Pandavs instead of siding with Duryodhan against his own brothers. Krishna told him that, since he would be the eldest Pandav, Yudhishthir would hand over the crown to him. Karn stayed loyal to Duryodhan.

A combination of factors led to Karn's defeat and death. Karn had promised to never refuse alms to a beggar who approached him during his midday sun worship. Before the battle, Arjun's father, the god Indra, approached Karn in disguise and asked for his impenetrable armor as alms. Karn's father, the Sun God Surya, had warned Karn about Indra's plans, but Karn chose to keep his promise. Kunti extracted a promise from him that he would not kill any of her sons except Arjun. On the sixteenth day of battle, Karn defeated Bheem, Yudhishthir, Nakul and Sahdev, but spared their lives. On the seventeenth day, Karn dueled with Arjun. At a crucial point, a curse made him forget the incantation which would give him his most powerful weapon. Karn called a halt to the battle so that he could get his chariot wheel out of the mud it was stuck in. Arjun, violating the rules of combat, attacked Karn with arrows and killed him while he was trying to move the wheel out of the rut.

Though Karn was associated with some of the Kauravs's dastardly acts, he is admired for his generosity and for honouring his word. Karn is seen as the great tragic hero of the *Mahabharat*. Karan remains a popular male name in India, and the town of Karnal in the state of Haryana is named after him. Legend has it that the Chhath Festival, which is celebrated by natives of a large region around Karn's erstwhile kingdom of Anga, originated in Karn's sun worship. The motif of brothers trapped in opposing sides of a conflict is common in popular culture, for example in the cult Hindi film *Deewar* (1975).

I

M I TOO heavy for you?' I asked her. 'No. I like your heaviness,' Vrushali replied.

I took my knees off the mattress and covered her hands and legs with mine. I liked pinning her down. She giggled, and I enjoyed the quivering of her soft, warm flesh. Her breath was still ragged, and we were still drenched. I took in the sweet smell of our sweat, and I thought about the many women I had been with from the time much before I became a king, starting with that first, clumsy effort in the jungle with Mala when I had erupted as soon as she cried out. My abilities improved with time, and so did the quality of my beds—from the floor of my hut in the village to this one, actually made of wood and embellished with a soft mattress which aided our frenzied lovemaking, in my mansion on the main street of Hastinapur.

I had known from the moment I fixed my eyes on Vrushali that all the others were part of a design to make me good enough for her. When she accepted me, it was the first time for her—and for me. For the first time, I felt the need to cling on after making love. She accepted me when things were not easy for me, when

I was still going through the pain of becoming a king, of fearing taunts about being a charioteer's son at best, perhaps worse, and an illegitimate child for sure.

Duryodhan was astounded when I told him, with a stammer, that I would not share a slave girl with him, that I would be loyal to the princess who had taken me into her body, her heart and her life after another princess had humiliated me in public. It was not the way of Kings, he had said, but I was free to choose my own path, and who knew, he added with a smile, perhaps my way was better than his.

I slid down so that I could listen to Vrushali's heart, the only one whose beats I knew. The beats came in pairs, like a slowed-down thudding of a horse's hooves. It reminded me of a dream I had had once too often. I was riding a white horse in a bluish haze, with my sword drawn, approaching a rider on a black horse. From the silhouette, I knew it was Arjun. I breathed through my mouth, and the icy wind had a salty taste. I sweated, and my hand grew clammy. I knew my grip on the sword was not strong enough. But I was committed. There was no stopping, no going back, no next time in this life. Our eyes met, and our gazes locked. We were at full gallop, but time had slowed down. And then, I could see the hairs on his wrist, there was a blur and I felt the sword slipping out of my hand and the rush of air as I fell. The fall would wake up me, and I would feel a numbing relief first, before the self-reproach set in.

When it became too much for me, I went back to the jungle and to my guru, Virsa. We sat at the cliff edge with our feet dangling down. He had listened impassively, though I would not hold it against him if he showed contempt.

'There is this thing called fear,' he said, after sucking the nectar of a red flower and smacking his lips. 'The brave know it. A warrior who does not feel it is a fool who will fall easily. If it makes you sweat, and your breath quick and shallow, you will be weak. But if you accept it with calm, it will make you stronger.'

'Did the dream have a meaning?' I asked. 'Why were we fighting with swords instead of arrows?'

He stretched in a fluid move, lay on his back and grinned. He looked long and hard at me. 'Dreams have meanings,' he said, 'but it is not for us to try to get at them.'

Then he turned serious. He said the one thing I must keep in mind was that when the conflict finally came, there would be one moment of truth that would pass in a blink. The years of training, the smouldering hate, would be irrelevant. In that moment, a few moves would decide who would win and who would die.

'Fear might even help the winner. Every mother's son feels fear.' He had smiled and added, 'and you, who have two mothers, the one who threw you into the river and the one who brought you up, perhaps it is all right for you to feel a little more.'

'What are you thinking?' Vrushali asked, bringing me back to the moment.

I sighed. What might she have been thinking? Perhaps about making tomorrow more pleasant. Anyway, I only had to ask and she would tell me. And here I was, with my head on her breast, thinking about war. Though I would never say it, for it was not a thought befitting a king, I did suspect that women have more civilised thoughts than men. I sometimes thought that if only every man could get a willing woman under him when he felt the need, there would be much less crime in the world. Kings would still make war, of course, but war is no crime.

She pressed herself upwards to prod me.

'I was thinking, I feel like a king when I am on top of you,' I lied.

'Not again!' She said. 'How can you take so much time to think so little?'

'I gave you a summary.'

'It's so hard to be with you. You don't perfume yourself, you don't wear silk robes, you hardly ever talk. You say one word for ten of mine. And you keep brooding. About all those things, about who said what, who threw you into the river when you were a baby. You keep thinking! And you never tell me what you're thinking.'

I manoeuvred to keep both her hands pinned with my left hand, and tickled her armpit with my right. 'That's how I am.'

She shrieked and tried to wriggle out from under me, but it was no use. 'Get off me then!' she commanded.

I could read her face in the dim light. Her eyes had the crinkles which told me she wasn't really angry. I licked her armpit and pinched her breast. She managed to get an arm free, pulled my ear, sank her nails into my shoulder and disentangled from me. She had grown fond of pulling my ears ever since I told her that I felt a bit embarrassed about how long they were. The marks on my shoulder would show in the day, and Duryodhan would have a wisecrack ready. I sat up cross legged, stretched, and reached out for the lamp. I held it and admired her while she lay there panting. I liked looking into her large brown eyes.

'Why don't you loosen up a bit, King Anga?' 'I like looking at you this way.'

'Now you're changing the subject.'

I reached out and tickled her feet. 'What was the subject?'

'What ... were ... you ... thinking?' She shouted out.

I flinched. 'Not so loud,' I whispered. 'You weren't scared when I screamed.'

'Did you say scared?'

She sat up, cross legged like me, leaned forward and gave me a peck on my mouth. She took the lamp from me and put it away. 'Of course not, you are never scared, right? You can beat Arjun at archery, you can look at the sun forever without being blinded, you know the scriptures better than Yudhishthir, you can swim across the river and back in the twinkling of an eye, and you killed a snake when you were eight, and a tiger when you were twelve.'

'Are you making fun of me?'

She sighed and stroked my forehead. I lay down with my head in her lap. I liked that view of her breasts. She let her hair fall on my chest.

'Do you think I would do that?'

'No.'

'No,' she mimicked me. She continued her caresses. 'Do you know what your problem is? You torment yourself too much. Why don't you just look at how far you have come and feel happy about it?'

'Do I look unhappy?'

She smiled. 'No, but you keep brooding. Tell me what you were thinking?'

'I wish my parents lived with me.'

'That's a lie,' she said.

'What?'

'I mean, I know you wish your parents lived with you, though I don't know if you would make me scream if they were in the mansion. That's not what you were thinking.'

I felt a calm descend on me as I prepared to sleep. I took her hand in mine and kissed it. 'A king must keep his thoughts to himself,' I said. 'Can you put me to sleep, please?'

'What a clever man you are,' she said, smiling, as she stroked my forehead, just above the eyebrows, with the thumb and index finger of her right hand. Sleep had almost found me when the bell outside started to peal. I woke with a start, and she sighed. 'Oh, the burdens of Kingship,' she mocked me.

I stood up and reached for my clothes. 'Will you step out in that condition?'

I looked down, and looked at her, and my condition grew more acute. 'I'll imagine something ugly on the way. Like Bheem's face.'

She burst out laughing, and gave me a big hug.

It was true. I knew that all I needed to do to lose it was to step out of my chamber and ponder about matters in Hastinapur. I patted her, draped my robe, and walked toward the main gate. I drew my robe tighter as I crossed the door. The cold was biting.

'Victory to the Raja!' The two guards at the entrance to the main building said. It had taken me a while to get used to the obsequiousness of the guards. Vrushali taught me to accept it as a natural due, like the air that I breathed. I had found it easier to stare down the Kings whose company Duryodhan had catapulted me into, knowing I was smarter and stronger than them. I had to be, to get this far.

'Who disturbs me at this time?' I asked. The trick was to keep my voice level and low, and to not look at them. They would latch on to every word, as if their lives depended on it.

'Sir, it is a messenger from the palace. We tried to stop him, but he says it is important. You have been called.'

I stood there and focused my hearing on the sounds of the night. The loudest sound was my own breathing. Here in this city full of life, the night was deathly quiet, unlike in the forests where I had acquired many of my skills. I felt the numbing cold of the earth seep through my sandals.

It was a half-moon night, and the light was just about enough to make out a figure crouched near the bell which I had got installed at the main gateway to the compound. The idea was that anyone who needed to see me could use it to call me. It had got me talked about, and it gave me another channel to my people, of whom there was a small but steady stream—mostly traders—who travelled the long distance from Anga to Hastinapur.

I walked to the gateway with deliberately slow steps. The messenger was still sweaty. He shivered in the cool air. In my earlier life, I would have given him something to cover himself with. I stopped a few paces away from him.

'Victory to the King,' he said, and bowed and did a namaste. I looked at him and he lowered his eyes. His face was familiar.

'They have called you, Sir. They said you should come now. I can take you there.'

'Who?'

'Prince Duryodhan and Minister Vidur.'

I turned back and looked up at the window, which was softly lit. 'Get the chariot,' I said. Duryodhan insisted that I must always have a charioteer, and never be seen driving a chariot myself in Hastinapur. The Pandavs could easily get someone to make a jibe about it.

II

THE STREETS OF Hastinapur were deserted. I had never seen them at this hour. Vrushali had given me a woolen shawl to wear and insisted I wear my helmet. It was just as well. As I stood in the chariot, the wind numbed my nose. I realised that I had softened a bit since I moved into the palace. This would not do. I decided to spend a few nights on my own in the jungle, and, of course, the thought of missing Vrushali came to mind. I pushed it away gently. The breath of the horses made smoky shapes in the weak light, and the reflections of street lamps shimmered on the surface of the canal in the middle of the royal avenue.

The guards at the palace gates saluted me, and I ignored them. The gates were flung open so that the chariot did not have to slow down. It flew the flag of Anga. The man drove all the way to the meeting hall next to the main audience hall. The door was wide open, and the hall was fully lit. I dismounted without waiting for the driver to come around and place his hand for me to step on. My sandals knocked loudly on the wooden steps which led to the hall.

A shadow moved into the patch of light cast by the door on the steps. It was Duryodhan. He wore a red shawl that was so fine it didn't even look woolen. He welcomed me with half a hug. His eyes weren't smiling.

'Brother, that was fast,' he said.

I loved it when he called me his brother. He called his real brothers by their names. 'The streets were empty,' I said to him. 'Pranam, Minister.' This I said to Vidur who stood in the centre of the hall. He joined his hands in a namaste without changing his expression.

'Is all well?' I asked.

'If it was…' Vidur started to speak, but stopped and sighed.

'Ambassador Brahmdutt has been murdered,' Duryodhan said. 'You know him. Or knew him. Whatever. It's a curious case. I was one of the last people to see him. I did go to see him, and I have been discussing with him that Shri Balaram's support for me will make things easier for all of us.' We walked toward Vidur.

That explained the urgency, I figured. Ambassador Brahmdutt was Kushasthali's ambassador to Hastinapur. More importantly, he was Shri Balaram's aide. As Krishna's elder brother, Balaram's endorsement could make a huge difference to Duryodhan and me. It would neutralise Krishna's support for the Pandavs, and perhaps sway Krishna to a neutral position. It could even put an end to the talk of a great war.

I took all this in and shrugged. 'It appears that the murder has something to do with my being summoned here. At this late hour.'

'Do you think your time is more valuable than ours?' Vidur asked. His face remained stoic, but his voice rose.

Now we three faced each other. Duryodhan frowned, and I knew he might explode.

'May the gods grant peace to Brahmdutt's soul,' I butted in. 'I have no such illusions about the relative values of our time, I assure you.'

I thought I must put in a word with Duryodhan separately. It would not do for him to antagonise Vidur. It was enough that Vidur hated me.

'Let me explain this,' Vidur said in his measured way. 'The Pandavs are out in Kripa's gurukul. Brahmdutt did tell me that he had his men do a survey. It seems that the popular sentiment is that Yudhishthir will make a better king. He also said that this would be his message to Balaram. It might not make a difference to Balaram, as he has his own ways. I understand he wishes to stay neutral, because he loves both you, Duryodhan, and Bheem.'

Duryodhan nodded. I had learned much from him, especially economy of words and movements. I liked the way he exuded authority, just standing there with his hands folded. Of course there were rare moments when his patience ran out, and then he could go berserk.

'Anyway,' Vidur continued, 'Brahmdutt lived alone, except for a serving girl, and he retired to his mansion well before sunset. Duryodhan knocked loudly on his door a little after he retired and spent some time with him. According to the serving girl's report, when she went to his room in the evening she found the door bolted. She called out, but there was no reply. She thought he might have some secret work going on and let it be. When she checked again, late at night, the door was still bolted. She ran out to call the night sentry, who broke the door down and discovered the body. It appears that he was first clubbed with a mace, and then stabbed in the chest. The curious thing is that the room was closed from inside.' He waited for me to speak. I must have shown my surprise, but I kept quiet.

'I know that Duryodhan has not done anything wrong,' Vidur said. 'I know. But that is not how things work. As Balaram's aide, Brahmdutt's disappearance in this manner is something which can shake the foundations of Hastinapur. I do not need to tell you about the fallout of antagonising Balaram. The consequences will not be good for you both.' I looked at Duryodhan. If Vidur had expected him to be defensive, he would have been disappointed. Duryodhan nodded in consent.

'You know'—and he looked at me when he said this—'that I do not approve of the way in which all traditions have been broken and you have been rapidly promoted by Duryodhan. I think he has made a mistake. Tonight, I cannot turn to Duryodhan's brothers. They will not be seen as neutral. The secret service itself will be seen as biased, and it is one of my mistakes that I did not work to change this impression. Of course, I did want the secret service to be feared more than loved.' He smiled. I wondered if he knew how ugly he looked. I had to admit though, that he had charisma.

'On the other hand, you are a good politician. With your gestures, your tendency to make promises and keep them, your donations, your sun worship, you have become popular. I know that the men on the streets think highly of you. And the women. If you do the investigation, people will believe it was fair, and you will have a chance to clear Duryodhan of blame, which should be enough reason for you to take this task.' He looked at me with raised eyebrows, as if he was challenging me to respond with anger. I smiled back at him.

'Will you take it?'

'In brief, yes,' I said.

Vidur tilted his head to his right and looked askance at me. 'Feel free to expand your answer a bit,' he said.

'There is nothing more to say at this stage. I will investigate on my own, and I will not be answerable to anyone.'

'That is absurd,' Vidur replied. I fondled the hilt of my sword.

Duryodhan placed his hand on my shoulder. 'You have to be answerable to the senior minister, Brother.'

'I meant no one except you, of course,' I said, looking at Vidur.

'Of course,' he said.

Duryodhan saluted Vidur and started to walk away. I would have done the same, but Vidur placed his hand on my shoulder and squeezed it. Duryodhan looked at us, shrugged and walked on.

'I wanted to talk to you,' Vidur said. 'I have been meaning to do it, but this is finally a good time.' This was curious. 'You know, it is hard to explain, but what you need to know is that I admire you.'

I was shocked, and it must have shown.

'Yes, I don't show it. You see, my story is a bit like yours.' He glanced at the door to confirm that Duryodhan was out of earshot. 'I have carved out a path for myself against the odds. I did not have lineage. Or let me put it this way, I had known mixed lineage, and you have unknown lineage which may or may not be better than mine. It's hard to say who is better off.' He shrugged and smiled wryly.

I stayed quiet.

'I know I have been hard on you, since the time you first challenged Arjun, and after that. The thing is— and you only have my word for it—that I very much want you to succeed. From a larger perspective, our society will only benefit if it is more meritocratic. That is our point, yours and mine. Believe me, I try to appear harsh on you so that when I praise you I am not seen as an upstart helping another one.' He chuckled. 'It just works better this way.'

I burst out laughing. 'I thought you and Rajmata Kunti were the ones who hated me the most!'

Vidur closed his eyes. He seemed to be working out what to say next. 'You were wrong.' He turned his head to one side and was lost for some more time. Then he sighed and continued. 'On this case, you must do justice to your reputation. I will sleep easier if you say you will. You don't have to promise me. I know—'

'I promise you, Sir.' I interrupted him. My words came out a bit hoarse. I saluted him and he broke into a weathered grin. It had character, that pockmarked face of his.

'You will have to get started now,' he said, 'there is no time to lose.'

I saluted him. When I turned around and walked away into the cold, my shadow moved out of his and became longer.

III

WE HAD TAKEN A short cut. The wheels of the chariot creaked on the uneven surface of the side streets. We moved slower, and the streets were narrower, and the cold was less biting. The bumpiness of the ride helped, as well, to keep me warm. I was thinking about the events of the night and trying to put a face to the name of Brahmdutt. The horses neighed, and the chariot lurched to a stop. I would have fallen if I was not holding on to the pole. The man who had come for me was still driving.

He turned around with wide eyes and said, 'Forgive me, Sir! It's these new homeless people. I would have driven over them if I did not stop.' He was trembling, and his voice quavered. 'It is dark. I am sorry.'

I could make out some huddled shapes moving on the side of the street. 'What do you mean, homeless?'

'They have no homes, Sir.'

I tried to figure this. 'How can that be?' The shapes behind him had morphed into men, about five that I could make out.

'I do not know much about it, Sir. I hear that there is less money because of the war talk. Who am I to talk about these things, Raja?'

'So now there are men without homes? In Hastinapur?' It was interesting that there could be men, in this age and in this land, without homes. In Hastinapur, of all places. I beckoned the shapes toward me. They moved very slowly. The first of the men on the street lowered the cloth draped around his head. He peered with bleary eyes, first at me, and then at the flag, and froze. He was down on his knees the next instant.

'Raja, we …,' he trailed off and looked behind him. The others were on their knees as well. 'We have nowhere to go, Sir,' he said, looking at me. 'We came here to search for a living, but, … We are sorry to hold you up, Sir.'

I put a foot on the railing of the chariot, and my arm on my thigh. This was really curious. 'Are you all able-bodied?'

'Well, Sir, the body is able, yes,' another man said. 'That's a way of putting it, but we are not able to feed it.' This was one of those at the back. The one in front looked alarmed.

I motioned with my finger to the one who had spoken, and he came forward, hobbling on his knees. 'What can you not do?' I asked.

'Raja?'

'What's hard to understand?' I raised my voice just enough to menace him. 'Are you unable to walk? To run? To lift a load? To plough? Are you disabled in any way?'

'Raja, no, apart from being tired and hungry losers, there is nothing wrong with us. We can do work, but we have got none.'

I asked the driver to light a torch, and he did it. One of the horses neighed. The breath of the horses formed misty conical plumes. I could see now that the man was quite tall. His eyes were clear, not shifty. Like his mates, he had a rough piece of cloth wrapped around himself.

'And there are five of you in the city?' I asked.

'Sir, there were six of us, and one disappeared— we do not dare to ask the kottapal to trace him. But in the city there are dozens. There may be hundreds before long. Not on the royal avenue, of course. No offence meant, Sir.'

I knew I could lash out at him and he would take it with the meekness of the loser, but I liked his spirit. There was something about this man.

'Do you know who I am?' I asked very softly. 'Yes-yes, Raja, Sir.' He folded his hands.

I straightened up and stretched. This homelessness phenomenon was very new for me. There was so much to learn. A door opened to our left, and a man stepped out with a lit torch. He opened his mouth to harangue us, but stopped open-mouthed. I ignored him.

'All right. Here is what you will do. You will go to my palace tomorrow and ring the bell there. In the room, on the right of the compound, there is an officer. He will give each one of you three packets of grain and two coins. He will give you directions to Anga. It will take you a few full moons to get there, perhaps three. If any one of you wastes the money on women and wine, I will find out and have you all traced and killed.' They gesticulated to show me that that was out of the question.

'Once you are in Anga,' I said, 'you will follow my officer's instructions and train to join my army. Your stomachs will be full, you will have homes, and you can do what you like with your pay.'

They knelt there in silence.

'Well? Am I clear or not?' I asked.

'Raja, we cannot believe this,' said the man I had called forward. 'We had heard great things—'

'That's enough!' I cut him short. 'Spread the word. I would like more men. I have no use for only the five of you. If I see any one of you homeless lingering on here, unless he has a disability, there will be trouble for him.' I paused to let the threat sink in. 'Is that clear?' I asked.

'Raja …,' someone at the back started hesitantly and stopped.

'What is it?' I was brusque.

The man cleared his throat first, and then said, 'We are not warrior caste Kshatriyas.'

'You do know who I am?' I asked.

'Yes, Raja, of course, the people really—'

'That's interesting. Even I don't know myself. Yet. Get out of the way now. And remember, do not cheat me.'

They got out of the way double quick, and we continued. I did not look back and pretended to ignore the warm words of the homeless men. It had grown colder. My flesh had goose bumps, and I blew clouds of misty breath which were quickly dispersed as the chariot moved forward. We turned on to a wider street, closer to the river bank, where the ambassadors had their residences. The chariot lurched to a stop in front of one of the residences, the only one with lamps burning. I jumped off the chariot before it stopped completely.

Three figures were silhouetted in the brightly lit door. My eyes watered a bit from the cold. I took in the gateway at the entrance to the garden. The mansions on the street were all similar in size and appearance, but the other gateways were not as ornate as this one. Each of the buildings was single-storied and surrounded by a garden. The plots were about a hundred metres wide. The gardens did not have high trees and were demarcated by stone walls about two metres high. This one had a smaller annexe—it had to be a toilet—on the right side, which was adjacent to the next building's annexe.

I strode toward the door. It was a relief to feel the surge of warmth as I crossed the threshold, even though the bright light was a bit disorienting. The three figures bowed and saluted me. There were two men, obviously sentries, and a girl who must be the serving girl. She was unusually fair—I preferred dark women—but her curves were pleasing to the eye, and they were accentuated through her shawl when she bowed. I felt a bit irritated that my gaze lingered on them, but by then I had figured that the animal part of me was not going anywhere. It was all right, as long as the human part dominated it. The thing to note was that the serving girl was alluring. That might have something to do with the case.

'You two are the sentries on this street, are you?' I asked. 'And you are Brahmdutt's serving girl?'

They nodded. The serving girl spoke first, 'Yes, Raja. They sent a man to tell us to wait here till you arrived.'

'Let's go to the sleeping room,' I said. They followed me as I walked past the hall and entered the cold and dark courtyard. In the moonlight, I made out two doors each on my right and left. I walked on briskly and pushed open the damaged doors of the sleeping room. The first thing which struck me was its sheer size. Brahmdutt had apparently got two rooms joined. I looked at the huge fourposted bed on the left side of the room. There were dark brown splatters of blood all over the bed sheet. I walked over and stroked a clean patch. It was silky smooth. I imagined—what else—the serving girl writhing on it. I gently pushed the thought away and replaced her image with Vrushali's. I wondered if I should be so pleased with my rectitude. The girl was right behind me. The two sentries stood at the door, shivering, reluctant to come in. I signalled to them to come in and shut the door behind them.

The wooden walls of the room were mostly bare, except for a row of weapons on the right side, a human-sized statue of a dancing girl with impossible, and therefore very pleasant, proportions on the left. A large cupboard ran along the back wall, behind the bed. Two identical, large windows, each about a meter square, framed the left and right sides. The windows were barred with wooden slats. Two smaller windows in the back had their solid-looking bolts closed. I walked over to them, one by one, reached out and flipped their bolts open and shut a few times. It took some effort. These windows looked out on a garden with some vegetable plants, a small structure which would be the stable, and the rear boundary wall. Beyond the wall there was the river embankment. Above the embankment, I could see a slice of the river.

I went to the windows on the sides, and tested the slats one by one. They held firm, each one of them.

I turned to the three of them and said, 'Tell me what happened, one by one. You first.' I pointed to the serving girl. 'What is your name?'

'It is Amba, Raja. I went to serve the master, but he didn't open the door when I knocked, and then I went much later, and he still didn't. Then I ran to the sentry, this man,' she started and was about to go on.

I motioned her to stop. 'Tell me bit by bit. You say you went to serve him, and he did not open the door when you knocked? When was that? Take a deep breath before talking. Be calm. I can hear you if you speak half as loud as you did.'

She blushed. 'The sun had just set.'

'How much time after Prince Duryodhan left? Did you see him leaving?'

'The Prince left at sunset. I took water for them, and then they talked. I heard his chariot leaving at sunset, just after that the master closed the sleeping room door.'

'Where was Brahmdutt's chariot all this time? Was it used during the day?'

'He went out for some time in the afternoon, yes.' Her tone, and her breath, was more measured now. 'He returned and drove the chariot right to the door of the house. He usually leaves it outside the gateway, where yours is parked now.'

It struck me that I had missed this bit. I remembered that there were hoof marks and wheel tracks going right up to the door. 'Was he driving it himself then?' I asked.

'Yes Raja, he drives himself.'

'And you saw it being driven all the way in?'

'No Sir, I only saw it parked right outside, but I didn't see him driving it in.' The girl was more confident and measured now. Why had she been so flustered?

It took me a while, and a few iterations with the sentries, to put the story together. Duryodhan had left at sunset, and some of the discussion was loud enough to be heard in the serving girl's room. Duryodhan had said Brahmdutt was twisting the voice of the people, and that he should be careful. That sounded ominous. Brahmdutt had, of course, seen him to the gateway. Amba saw them walking to the door, and she saw Brahmdutt return alone.

She went to Brahmdutt's room a little after sunset with a pitcher of sura wine. The meeting room was empty, and the sleeping room was locked. There was no reply when she knocked on the sleeping room door. This was unusual, but it had happened earlier that Brahmdutt would lock himself in when he did not wish to be disturbed.

Amba went to check a little later—she could not say how much later—and Brahmdutt still did not respond. Now this was strange. Amba called out, and did not know what to do when Brahmdutt did not reply. She left the wine pitcher and tumbler on the courtyard floor and paced about for some time. Then she knocked again. Finally, she ran out. The street lamps were lit, but the street was deserted. She would have run to the next mansion, which belonged to the ambassador of Dwarka, but she saw the sentry making his rounds. She ran to him and breathlessly explained the problem. The sentry and the serving girl ran in together to the mansion, calling out to Brahmdutt. When he did not reply, the sentry broke open the door with some effort. His right shoulder bore bruises, and his sword had left marks on the frame where he had used it as a lever.

When they got in, they saw Brahmdutt lying on his bed with his face bashed in, a dagger stuck in his chest, and blood dribbling out of the wound. The sentry sensed that Brahmdutt was quite dead. He turned to Amba and told her to run to the next crossing and call for his colleague, who was on the rounds there. She had collapsed on the floor, screaming incoherently. The first sentry did not remember her exact words. Anyway, there was no choice for the sentry but to leave her there and run to fetch help. He alerted the caretaker at the next mansion and also got to the second sentry. This second sentry first told a colleague to cover for both of them, ran to the palace, requested a doctor and also informed the kottapal. The first sentry was back in the room very soon. He could not say how much time he took, but it was not too much. The serving girl sat on the floor where he had left her, still babbling and dazed.

The doctor came in about a mahurt, which was not bad considering it was quite late. He took one look and pronounced Brahmdutt murdered, not by poisoning, but by clubbing and stabbing. He insisted on an identification mark, and was satisfied when Amba pointed toward his feet, which had six toes each. The duty officer at the kottapal's office also got there in a while. He said that the murder needed to be investigated, but as the doctor was confident about the cause of death, there was no need to delay the cremation. The body was wrapped and taken to the river ghat by city council workers.

While all this was going on, the two sentries checked all the windows. The ones on the side were barred, and the rear window was locked from inside. There was no one under the bed, of course. The sentries tapped the floor and the roof. They could not make out any secret passages. The weapons lined up on the side wall were not bloodied. There were two silver coins and some of Brahmdutt's jewellery in the cupboard.

Each sentry patrolled the length of six mansions on the well-lit street. As the sentries marched in tandem, one of the adjoining sentries would have had the front of Brahmdutt's mansion in his view when the first sentry had his back to it—in principle, at least.

I talked to the three of them together, and separately, and realised after some time that I had all the detail I needed. Brahmdutt's body was at the cremation ghat close by. I dismissed the first sentry, told Amba that I would be back, and asked the second sentry to accompany me to the ghat with a torch.

We stepped out into the cold. I motioned to the charioteer that he should stay where he was. The sentry followed me down the street, which was now deathly quiet, carrying a torch. The earth was damp, and my soles quickly became wet. I thought through the whole sequence of events on the way.

'Was there a chariot inside the house, at the door, when you went in?' I asked the sentry.

'No, Raja,' the sentry said. His teeth were chattering. 'It was in the back, and the horse was in the stable.' There was something about the chariot being driven to the door, and then to the back. If I drove the chariot myself, I would leave it outside the main gateway if I planned to use it again. If I was done for the day, I would take it straight to the back of the house.

At the ghat, there was only one shrouded body on a pyre. I told the sentry to get the priest. He headed toward the temple compound across the embankment, taking the torch with him. The torch had probably not warmed us much, but I felt colder without it.

The river was wide here. I looked toward Brahmdutt's mansion. There was nothing much to distinguish it from all the others, except that it still had some lamps lit. I could only see its roof protruding above the embankment. On the other side, the river flowed quietly, with a sliver of white where it reflected the half-moon.

Brahmdutt had been a power centre in Hastinapur—powerful enough for me to have at least heard his name—and here he was now, bundled in a shroud, all alone. If his day had been uneventful, he would have been enjoying the company of the serving girl now instead of being cremated by an official for whom the corpse would be another mass of tissue to be consigned to the flames.

The sentry returned with the priest. The priest greeted me with deference.

'Is that it?' I asked him.

He nodded.

'Remove the shroud,' I ordered.

The priest did it. I shuddered at the sight. The sentry rushed to a corner of the steps and retched. The doctor could not have done much about his face. It was bashed in. At least he had been clothed properly. The gash on his solar plexus was no uglier than I expected. I checked that he had a sixth toe on each foot, as the serving girl had told me.

'It is kind of you to take the trouble at this time, Raja,' the priest said.

'It is duty.' I said.

'His spirit will be grateful that of all people, you agreed...'

'Yes. I will try to sort this out. When will he be cremated?'

'We do not have to wait, Sir, since you have been kind enough to come.'

'What does that have to do with it?' My words came out a bit louder than I wanted.

The priest cringed. 'As you know, Sir, his wish was to be cremated by you. He had come only a few days ago. Who could have thought...' He stopped halfway through his thought.

'I have come here to investigate the crime. What is all this about my cremating him?'

The priest was hesitant. 'Raja, he had come by, and he said that he feared for his life. He was worried that he had no one to cremate him, and he expressed a wish that if he was to … pass away, he wanted to be cremated by you.'

'What? When did this happen?' I asked.

The priest stepped back, alarmed. 'Sir, two-three days—'

'Two or three?' I asked. His hands were trembling. It must have been from the cold.

'Two, Sir.'

'So, he walked in and said this? To you? Is this usual?'

'No Raja, it is not, but it happens once in a while. If they have no son to cremate them, they often express what should be done, perhaps with their ashes. Or they ask for a priest from their part of the country to cremate them, if possible.'

'Once again, he asked for me to cremate him?'

'Yes, Raja, he was very clear. I was there. I told him, well, that if it happened, we would convey the request and then it would be up to you.'

'And you did not ask why he chose me?'

'He only said that he would consider himself blessed. He said he is … was … a modern man and he did not care about pedigree—' here he flinched and stopped again. 'I am sorry. I mean that he respected you a lot. That's what he said, Raja.'

A little later, we watched the fire consume the shrouded body. It built up slowly, and then there was a moment when it roared and the flames leapt up so high and fierce that we had to step back. I felt guilty about basking in the warmth of the fire, but I couldn't bring myself to move away till the fire had spent itself and collapsed into a seething mass of embers. All this while, the questions kept coming to me. Someone whom I didn't know walked into the ghat and asked that I cremate him if he died. Then, he was murdered. The room in which he was murdered was locked from inside. The murdered person's advice could have tipped Balaram toward the Pandavs. Was there a thread connecting all these events? What were the chances there wasn't?

We walked back to Brahmdutt's house, the sentry and I. His torch had died out by now. The sky had turned lighter. I would have liked to stay back at the ghat to meditate while the sun rose, but there was still much to do. I had ordered the priest to send the urn with the ashes to my office, and to take the payment for the ghee and the wood later in the day. As I climbed up the steps of the ghat, my knees were a bit stiff. This would not do, I thought. I had to tone myself up. I had only missed a dinner and stayed up all night, and my body was already complaining.

The serving girl took quite a while to open the door when I knocked. She had draped her shawl tighter, and her eyes were half closed.

'Who dressed Brahmdutt for his funeral?' I asked as I strode into the visitors' hall.

She stifled a yawn. 'I did, Raja,' she said. 'The sentry was also there, but he could not help.' 'You did not feel ill while doing it?'

'I fainted. The sentry woke me up by sprinkling water.'

'So, you were there together?'

'Yes, Raja.'

'Where will you go now?'

'I do not know, Raja. I think Shri Balaram will decide when he visits next.'

'Did he wear any jewellery?'

Her eyes widened. 'Yes, of course, Raja. It is all here, I removed it.' She led me through the meeting room to the cupboard in the sleeping room, with slow steps. She opened one of the cupboard doors to show a necklace and a bracelet. They were gold; there was nothing extraordinary about them.

'He did not wear earrings?'

She looked at my gold hoops. 'No, Sir.'

I told her to send word through the sentry if she remembered anything unusual. The two sentries were mumbling to each other near the gateway. The charioteer was wide awake now. I climbed onto the chariot and dismissed the two sentries after telling them that I might summon them over the next few days.

The air was still chilly, but the darkness was retreating quickly. I told the charioteer to drive me home. Vrushali came running to the door when we entered the compound. I had to keep her waiting while I gave the driver instructions about messages to pass on to my officer, and to Duryodhan. I prayed to the rising sun to give me strength. When I finally reached the door I saw that her lips were stretched thin with anger, but her anger turned to worry when she saw me from closer. I held her and felt her warmth. She reached up and stroked my head.

IV

THE HEADQUARTERS OF the secret service were in a nondescript building off the royal avenue. It stood with a row of other two storied offices. If anything, its wooden pillars were a shade less polished. What did set it apart were the well-built guards at the doorway and along the passage which lead in. My right knee complained a bit when I jumped off the chariot. This would definitely not do, I thought. I walked coolly toward the two guards. I was not sure if they would stop me, and I kept my pleasure to myself when they stepped aside with effusive namastes.

It had been nice to feel the warmth of the sun on my back for a few moments. Inside, it grew progressively darker and damper as I walked toward the room of the duty officer. I could have sent word that I would visit, but I wanted to see how things worked without any oiling of the system.

The guards outside the duty officer's room stood apart immediately, and one of them looked over his shoulder at the officer. It was no use. The officer sat with his legs crossed on the platform, his elbow on his desk and his cheek nestled snugly in the ball of his palm. His eyes were closed and his breaths deep. I cleared my throat.

'Sir,' I called out from three arms lengths away.

He started and peered at me. It was nice and warm in the room. I couldn't really blame the man for dozing off. The fireplace to our right still had some smouldering embers, but the light was behind me.

'I am working on the murder of Brahmdutt, and I wanted some information,' I said.

The officer looked up and down at me, though it was probably wasted effort as he couldn't make out much. I had the light behind me. I could see that he was short but muscular. He had short curly hair.

He stifled a yawn, and said, 'Yes, leave a request with the guards outside, and we will let you know. If you guys in the police could read, it would be much better. But it's too late for you to learn. Come back tomorrow.' Something snapped in me. I imagined unsheathing my sword and bringing it down on his desk in one fluid move. Before I knew it, I had done just that. The officer's jaw dropped open. He reached for the hilt of his sword. To his credit, he was quick enough to draw it, but he froze when he looked at the guards behind me. I could see from the dance of the shadows that they were gesticulating vigorously. I pulled my sword back, but to my disappointment, the partition it had made in the desk was not completely smooth, at least not as smooth as it would have been with a saw. There was a scroll inside, which was neatly cut in two. As the officer scurried to one side, I turned to face him as I sheathed my sword.

His eyes dilated, and he seemed to recognise me. He clamped his jaw and stood there, scratching his curly head for a while. 'Sir, that desk has been with us since the time of King Shantanu,' he said in a slow, rustic accent which immediately warmed me. 'Anyway, you could have summoned us.' He shrugged. 'But of course, it is as you please. I hope you will arrange for it to be replaced? Hastinapur is not as rich as it used to be.'

I laughed, and the guards let out a collective sigh. 'I am sorry, I thought you were sleeping. I should have realised that you were contemplating the state of security in the city.'

'To be honest, Sir…'

'I'll replace the desk if you stay honest,' I said, and the three of them laughed. 'How many homeless men are there in the city?' I asked.

'One hundred and five this week, Sir,' he replied. 'They come and go, it depends.'

'And has this not been raised to the Palace?'

'Of course, it has, Sir, to Shri Vidur.'

'I see,' I said. 'Now I will step out and wait in my chariot. Send someone to report to me on this Brahmdutt murder. I have some questions about the people who were there at the spot. How much time will it take?'

'I, Meghnath, will come over myself, Sir,' the guard said. 'I will leave someone here. I know about the case, but I will take an update. About the desk…' He flinched.

'Raja, I know about your word. I am just not used to these things any more.' He grinned.

I fingered my earlobe, and then locked my fingers behind my head and cracked my knuckles. I quickly repeated what I wanted, and told him I would be waiting outside. My gut feeling about the man was right—he was out in less than a mahurt. I had spent the time thinking through what the serving girl and the two sentries had told me, while I luxuriated in the warmth of the morning sun. I ignored the people who stopped to stare, or to smile, at me.

I motioned to Meghnath to climb onto my chariot. He hesitated, and I gestured again. I figured I would more than make up for the scene in his office by inviting him up there with me. Anyway the best way to talk confidentially in this city was to be on my moving chariot. Even the charioteer would not be able to hear us. I became more and more impressed with Meghnath as he briefed me.

Brahmdutt was both a gambler and a money lender. He was suspected of pilfering some of the tribute from Kushasthali to Hastinapur. It had not been proved. The only way to establish it was to check a few things with Shri Balaram himself, and only Prince Duryodhan could do that. Brahmdutt was not married, and he had an enormous appetite for women and wine. He had got the serving girl, Amba, from Gandhar three years ago.

It was true that, as the serving girl had said, he had six toes on each foot. Brahmdutt had not left a will, and his estate would become property of Shri Balaram's kingdom of Kushasthali, probably being disposed of as Shri Balaram saw fit. He had refused to keep a charioteer, and for housework, he relied on three servants who visited the house during the day.

There was a time when there would be one sentry for every two houses on the street. With the budget under strain, those days had gone. However, between them, the three sentries on the street were likely to have seen any intruders. On the other hand, the riverside was less densely patrolled, because of the longer visibility. The river patrol consisted of two armed parties walking up and down the embankment. Much time, even two mahurts, could elapse between the two parties crossing Brahmdutt's house.

The first sentry was from a village nearby and had started service last week. So the chances of the two of them, this sentry and Amba, working in cahoots were low. The second sentry was from Kosala. He had been in service for a year. Brahmdutt received a steady stream of visitors, dozens per day. Duryodhan was the one visitor who stood out. It was otherwise impossible to get a record of visitors, as none was kept. Interestingly, the first sentry was seen talking to Bheem two days ago. And the sentry had come into money—he had visited a pleasure house on the day of the murder.

The case was still impossible to figure, but I realised I could not have dreamt of getting more information from Meghnath. I thanked him and dropped him back to the office and told him that he should stay in touch. He saluted me with a contented grin, and I parted with the knowledge that, on the whole, I had enhanced his standing in the city.

I felt a pang of hunger, since I had refused to eat before leaving home. I debated the options as the charioteer waited patiently. I could go home, but it was unlikely that I would slake only my hunger for food there. And time was of the essence. 'Drive me to the palace,' I commanded.

The doors were open for me. I walked in straight to Duryodhan's meeting room. Ignoring my protests, he dismissed the others as soon as he noticed me.

'You haven't slept or eaten since we met,' he said. He pulled on a bell-rope, and a serving girl appeared. He ordered two courses for me, fruits followed by meat. 'I hear you have been a bit innovative again?'

I had to think for a while. 'Do you mean about my taking the homeless men into my army?'

'They are not Kshatriyas, I am given to understand?'

'My trainers can make good soldiers out of women, Brother.'

Duryodhan smiled. 'I have no problem with it. Like I always say, your ways are different. And they may be better. If you are sure your army is not weakened, it's fine.'

'I think it is strengthened. When our forefathers— or at least yours—pushed the Nishads into the forest many seasons ago, they did not reserve military training for Kshatriyas. And we are not the only humans on the planet. If Mlechhas from beyond the Himalayas and the seas attack us, we will be weaker than them if we reserve fighting skills for a section of our men.'

Duryodhan frowned as he pondered that, caressing his biceps. 'It's interesting how you think. I have never heard the greatest strategists in my court talking like this. But anyway, what does it look like, the case?'

I had prepared on the way, and I told him everything. He took it all in without a word, without asking any questions. Then he paced about the room. He looked around warily, and said, 'Come up to the tower.' I had been very hesitant to go all the way up the first time. Now I looked forward to every opportunity. I must have been the only one from outside the royal families who was a regular there. I was tempted to tell Duryodhan that I would rather eat first, and I knew he would humour me if I did. I controlled myself. There would be time to eat later.

I knew that Duryodhan's favourite view was that of the city, the jewel of Aryavarta which had been snatched away from his father. He could see it all the way to the main gate at the end of the royal avenue. I liked to look across the palace grounds to the river. I had prayed to the sun once from here, and it was wonderful.

'Do you know the best thing about this?' He asked.

'The best thing?' I repeated.

'Yes, the bit about Bheem. Think about it! I am surprised you haven't already done it. The news of his being involved comes from the secret service without our prodding. All you have to do is to get it across to Shri Balaram that Bheem is somehow involved in this—he had been meeting with the sentry before the murder. I have met Brahmdutt, yes, but he was clearly alive when I left.' He screwed his eyes and flexed his right arm muscles.

'It's a small thing, but if we manage to use it right, and you know how Shri Balaram is, it doesn't have to be very logical. If we just keep it hazy and get Bheem implicated... Think about it! Shri Balaram on our side, maybe even Shri Krishna! This is it! We will be this close to sealing our victory.'

I must have recoiled.

'Look, you have to do this!' He frowned and gripped my shoulder. 'What's wrong?' He asked. My shoulder started to hurt.

'Are you crazy?' He had never raised his voice to me before that.

I could not look him in the eyes. 'Do you know what this means?'

'Even you don't, Brother,' I spoke softly.

'Don't call me brother!' His face was contorted, and he was shouting. Some of the palace guards looked up toward us.

I should have felt humiliated, but perhaps there was no time for all that to sink in. It took me a long time, I think, to look up at him, in the eyes. 'I suppose I should go now,' I said. I joined hands in a namaste.

He held his palm out toward me. 'Wait!' He was still loud and he was breathing fast and hard. He grabbed his long hair with his hands and pulled it.

'You are not in command of yourself, Prince,' I said. 'Stop that!' he shouted even louder and collapsed against the railing. He held his eyes closed for a while, and stood there, slouched and panting. 'You do not understand.' He was very soft now. 'You do not know what it is to be born here, to grow up knowing that this was yours, but it was taken away because your father was blind. He was wise enough, but that didn't help. And my mother—and how many times I have been taunted for being a blind man's son! And I really don't want to lose you, it's so hard to make friends after a certain age.' He straightened up and stood there with his arms folded.

'What can I say? I made a promise, you know, to Shri Vidur, to do justice, but even without it...'

'You and your promises!' He was going wild again. I looked around, at the guards down below peering our way. There couldn't have been a more public theatre than this.

'I have to refuse you, Sir,' I said.

'*You* refuse *me*?' he shouted again. Luckily that was the end of his screaming. He continued in a hoarse whisper. 'There will be blood, you know, rivers of blood. Think about it, think. Men will cremate their sons. And this man, a fool and thief, why do we even need to trace his murderer?'

'I have to leave, Prince,' I said. I did not need to pretend to be humble. It came naturally. I looked down at the silver inlay on the knobs of my sandals. How long would I wear them? And Vrushali? What would happen to us? I had asked her once if she would have married me if I was not a king. She had made a mock serious face and said that she loved me for the person I was—and that meant for being a king. As I took the stairs down, Duryodhan disappeared from my view. Just before he disappeared completely, I saw his eyes, wide and beseeching.

I ignored the guards on the way out, and told my charioteer to take me to the river, to the ghat near my mansion. It was less cold now, and I sat by the river for some time. I meditated with my eyes open, gazing at the midday sun. I enjoyed the moment when my third eye tingled. A little later I took a dip in the biting cold water. When I stepped out, I felt heavier and my steps were unsteady. I was hungry.

When I reached my mansion, Vrushali was at the door, looking pensive. The officer stopped me for some instructions, and I gave them mechanically.

'What have you done?' She asked in a broken voice when I got to her.

'What have you heard?'

She lowered her eyes. 'They say we will have to leave Hastinapur.' She had tears in her eyes.

I walked past her and changed into a new set of clothes. I still carried the shawl she had given me. She sat slumped in the meeting room. I heard her cry out to me, and I heard the charioteer say something. I did not bother to make meanings out of the voices. The charioteer stood stunned when I brusquely motioned him to one side and drove off on my own. I sensed Vrushali running out of the house and following me but stopping before the outer gate. The streets were quiet, and I drove at a furious pace, even lashing the horses. The guards at the main gate tried to say something, but I did not bother to slow down, and they had to open the gate for me.

I had brought a set of weapons apart from the sword which was always at my side, and I had the shawl to keep me warm. I had not thought about where I would go. Of course, home is wherever the doors are always open for you. For me, apart from my own mansion, that would be the place where Adhirata and Radha, whom I had only now started to call by their names, had brought me up after they found me abandoned in a small basket in the river. As it happened, our house there had no doors.

They had refused to live with me, because I had insisted on honouring them as my parents. Or was it because they wanted me to be king? Adhirata insisted that I would not be accepted as a king unless I was seen to be a king. We drifted apart even though we did not part ways.

Now, when I reached the fork for my village, I found myself driving past without slowing down. A little later, there was a less trodden path heading up into the hilly area. I turned into it. The path became narrower, and soon it was covered by a canopy of forest. I slowed down. My thoughts turned to Virsa, the guru who had given me much of my prowess. All of a sudden, I realised that at that point I wanted to see him more than anyone else. It was always easy to get to him. I would only have to reach any of the Nishads, and then activate their network.

I felt the earth tug at my left wheel and reined the horses. I brought the chariot to a halt, and the neighing of the horses pierced the drone of the cicadas. The left wheel was stuck in a patch of slush. I looked around. This part of the forest had been surrendered by the animals to us humans, and there would not be any snakes here. I still kept my sword by me as I stepped down, by force of habit. My shoulder hurt a bit as I got the wheel out of the rut.

A warm body leapt onto my back, wrapped an arm around my shoulder and neck, and blocked my eyes with a palm. I reached for my sword by reflex, but then I knew it must be one of the Nishad children, from the smell and the way the body racked with laughter. He climbed on my back and attempted the difficult task of hanging on, while blocking my eyes and also competing with me for my sword. It was easy for me to reach back and tickle his armpit. I got a loud laugh, and the child jumped off me on to a grassy patch. It was one of Virsa's boys. I kept tickling him, and he was in splits. I stopped when he was about to start crying. I smacked his butt and asked, 'What were you trying? Which one are you?'

'I got you!' His voice was surprisingly girlish. 'I will tell Father, right now.'

'Is he here then? Not in the cave?'

'Yes, he is here. I can take you. Let me drive!'

The path had narrowed to a grassy opening in the jungle, and the horses had become tentative by the time we stopped. The boy jumped and ran off into the undergrowth, and then turned around and asked, 'Why are you so slow, Long Ears?'

I smiled at him. I had to clear my throat before I could speak. 'I can't leave these here. Come and carry them for me.'

He bounded forward and picked up the bow and the quiver full of arrows. I untied the horses, and we mounted a horse each. His chest was puffed up as he led me on, with the quiver slung across his small shoulder, and he swayed a little more than necessary as he rode on with practised ease.

'Father! Look who has come! And I knocked him out!' He was shouting before we entered a clearing with a circle of huts.

Very soon there was a commotion, and I was embraced by at least a dozen people of all ages and both sexes as soon as I had dismounted. They had finished their meal of the day, so once again I was not lucky when it came to food. But I was glad to be back here, in a different world, with these people whose minds were so different. It was a while before I recognised Virsa in the melee and went over and touched his feet. I could not believe he had aged so fast. He was still muscular, but his hair had turned completely white, and his skin was mottled.

'Ah, it is you. You are thinking how much I have aged.'

'No one gets younger, Guru-ji, and the days go by slowly but the seasons go fast,' I said.

'And you come here only when you need us, when you are troubled beyond a limit.' He laughed, and I could not help noticing his decaying teeth. 'I have heard, anyway, that your might comes from training with one Parsuram, a thousand-year-old guru?'

I felt a tightening in my cheeks.

'Now don't blush!'

'Well, what can I say? It's not a story which I started, but when it spread it didn't do me any harm,' I said.

'And it would harm you to admit that you learned a few things from me?' He raised one eyebrow, and I joined hands and bowed in shame.

'Come now, we must test you against my eldest.' He frowned and looked hard at me. 'Is something wrong with you? What is this about this little fellow knocking you out?'

'Aah, nothing.' I shrugged. 'I was getting my wheel out of the mud.'

Virsa laughed. 'So you think it doesn't matter that you got taken by surprise?'

'It won't happen again,' I told him.

'I believe it won't,' Virsa said with a smile.

I told him I needed to rest. He stepped closer and looked at me with concern. 'Let's walk to the cliff,' he said. 'You will stay? Go back tomorrow?'

I nodded, and the boy jumped onto me again. The children's names started to come back to me. This one must be Sugana. I shook him off and smacked him on the butt again, and he danced away. Virsa and I walked toward the cliff. The earth here was red, and it had a bit of the smell of rusting iron. The path was only wide enough for us to walk in single file. Virsa was quiet as he led the way. When we got to the cliff's edge, it was magnificent. The river flowed about five arms below, and the not-so-fiery sun bathed it in a warm light. We sat on the edge. Virsa squatted in his usual style, prepared to suck on the red flower he had plucked on the way. I imagined how good it would be to get that drop of nectar into my dry mouth. He looked hard at me, and then handed the flower over to me. I closed my eyes and sucked on it. The sweetness was intense, exhilarating.

He was quiet, and so was I. I knew he would wait. When the words started to come out, there was no stopping them. I was not used to talking much. It was strange how I became a different person here. When I was done, I let my legs dangle on the edge and eased myself on to my back. The clear blue sky was framed by the trees behind us. Virsa had not spoken yet. I soaked in the warmth of the mellow sun and focused my hearing on the sounds around us: the rush of the water below, a bird call and the hum of the forest. I was already quite at peace.

'What do you think about the murder?' I asked him. 'In a closed room, and no weapons to be seen? How could it happen?'

'How this one happened I do not know,' he said. 'It is important that the man was both clubbed and stabbed. One should have been enough, no?'

He raised and lowered his eyebrows twice in quick succession. It reminded me of the old days, when he taught me much by asking me questions.

'A person can appear to be killed in a closed room in several ways. There is a room, which—because of this invention of your people, the door—is closed. A person is murdered. So there is a room, there is an act of murder and there are some actors. The room is real enough, I think, but the other things are all suspect. Is it really closed? Is the victim really who you think it is? Is it really a murder? Did it really happen after the room was closed and before the room was entered again?'

Virsa traced a square in the ground with his finger and looked thoughtful. He continued, 'There can be hidden passages. There can be an accident which looks like a murder. The victim may be compelled to kill himself. Up in the hills, in winter, it may be a suicide with weapons made of ice, which melted away. Or advanced weapons can be used, such weapons that may be manipulated from outside. Am I making sense?'

That was another old habit of his, to check if I was really listening. I nodded with vehemence.

'Or it could be that the person was dead before the room was closed, and some trick was used to close the room from outside. A thin blade through a hole, for example, can be used to kill a person inside a room. Of course, the murder may have happened later, after the door was opened. In this case, the victim is incapacitated, and the person who breaks open the door is the one who kills the victim.'

I sighed. 'All of these could happen. None of them look likely,' I said. 'Why do you think he asked to be cremated by me?'

'Who knows?' Virsa snorted. 'You will not solve all this lying on your back here. You will have to get your arse back to Hastinapur and talk to the people who were involved. Those sentries, the serving girl. The neighbours. Find out who suddenly came into money. Use the secret service. Take a thorough look at that house.'

I smiled at him. The sun was pale now, and the breeze carried portents of a chilly night. But I felt a warmth here. 'I am tired and hungry,' I said.

He stood up without an effort, without using his hands to prop himself. I got up as well, and followed him back to the settlement.

V

I TOOK IN THE morning air in deep, greedy breaths. On either side, the forest flowed by in streams of green. I sat comfortably on the charioteer's seat, instead of driving from the platform behind.

The night before, I had finally got a full meal of fish porridge, and I had slept a deep, tired sleep. I was awakened by a fall in my dream, and—as it often happened with me—the images of the dream had faded by the time I willed myself to throw off the rough quilt and step out into the biting cold. I only remembered that it wasn't the dream with the horses. With shivering hands, I had struggled to strike a flame for the torch. It felt good to be doing all this on my own. Starting at the crack of dawn, I had swum to the far side of the river and back twice, run up the slope to the cliff, done a complete set of exercises and prayed to the Sun. When I thought about the case, then, with the energy surging through me, I thought much better.

The forest started to thin, and I shifted back to the platform. Soon I was on the main road to

Hastinapur, wondering how I would be received at the main gate. When I got there, the guards stood to attention and saluted me. Once I was on the royal avenue, I slowed a bit.

I realised that I had not planned my steps exactly. That was all right. I turned the chariot toward the secret service building first. The guards parted as I started to walk in.

A voice boomed from behind: 'Victory to the King!' I turned around and saw that it was Meghnath, the officer whom I wanted to see. I gestured toward the sun, and he shrugged.

'King, the more I work, the more damage I do. So I work as little as possible.'

I burst out laughing, and he grinned like a schoolboy who had told a good joke. I had to restrain myself from putting my hand on his shoulder as we walked into the building. Perhaps I had been removed from my kingship? If I had, it would free me from many of these constraints. I did not want to ask about it, but the signals from the guards and from Meghnath did not seem to suggest that I was no longer King of Anga.

I did not have the option of getting him on the chariot. I waited till we were equally distant from the two groups of guards, and then stopped him and told him softly what I wanted to be checked.

'It is hard to say when my men will intercept them,' he said after thinking for a while. 'They will naturally travel to Anga through Ahichhatra and Shravasti, and it is unlikely that they have covered half the distance to Ahichhatra. I can send two carrier pigeons to my men along the way and do bisection searches to get my men to wherever they are. It will take a few rounds of pigeon flights, so if we are lucky we should have the information by the end of today. But I cannot say.'

'I can only repeat this,' I said. 'I will remember your help.' I nodded, patted him on the shoulder and went back to my chariot. I was about to step on to the charioteer's seat when I heard a shouted salute from behind. It was my charioteer. He was panting and sweaty. He must have come running all the way from my mansion. He fell at my feet, and then got up and took the reins. I climbed onto the platform at the back. The next stop had to be Brahmdutt's place. I knew I had to take a more thorough look at it.

I told the charioteer to stop a few mansions away, so that I could walk into the place without advance notice. I asked him to get a long rope for me. It was completely quiet as I took a circuit of the mansion and its garden. Its plan was quite standard. There was a gateway in the middle of the front boundary. If you stood in the gateway and looked at the mansion, it was in the centre of the plot, and the annexe with the toilets would be on your right.

The garden was mostly grass and a few neat plants and bushes. The main door of the mansion had two windows on either side, and it opened to the visitors' hall. After this, there was the courtyard, with two rooms on each side. The sleeping room faced the courtyard and had the four windows opening to the garden. There was a distance of about forty metres between the main east-west walls and those of the neighbouring mansions.

The charioteer was there with the rope. I took it from him and walked toward the main door. It opened before I could knock, and the serving girl stood before me, demure and downcast. There was something about her which made me uncomfortable, probably the lust which she seemed to awaken every time we met, and which I smothered resolutely. She did a namaste. I nodded and went in. It took me a while to get the measures of the mansion, inside and outside.

It was clear that there was no secret room. In the sleeping room, the floor was solid. The tiles of the roof above it were interlocked, and it would be a lengthy job to remove them. You could not clear a hole without breaking at least one of them. I asked for a ladder and climbed it to take a look at the roof. The tiles had the same extent of mossiness. I could see that they had not been moved around for a long time. The spaces just below the sleeping room windows were grassy, and there would be no footprints if someone had stepped on any of them. I cursed myself for not having checked all this when I had started the investigation. But it was true that it would not have helped if I had. And then, I could hardly have predicted the way events had unfolded.

I stood in the garden and smelled one of the white flowers. I did not know its name. I thought through the testimony of the serving girl and the sentries. If I

Streets and walkways are shaded. The
shortcut to Brahmdutt's house leads to the
narrower street in the southwest corner. The
steps in the ghats are not drawn to scale.

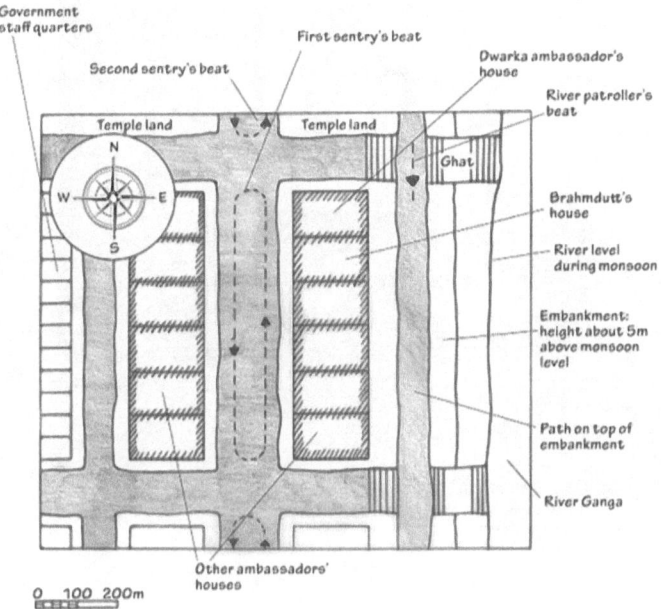

Government
staff quarters

First sentry's beat

Second sentry's beat

Dwarka ambassador's
house

River patroller's
beat

Temple land

Temple land

Ghat

N

W E

S

Brahmdutt's
house

River level
during monsoon

Embankment:
height about 5m
above monsoon
level

Path on top of
embankment

River Ganga

0 100 200m

Other ambassadors'
houses

Brahmdutt's neighbourhood

assumed they did not know each other, then the
implication was clear: the serving girl, the least likely
suspect, was the only one who had a few moments
with the corpse. She could not possibly have clubbed
and stabbed the victim to death. If she had poisoned
him first, he would not have bled so much. She could
not have removed the weapons, except to some hiding
place within the mansion. The important thing was

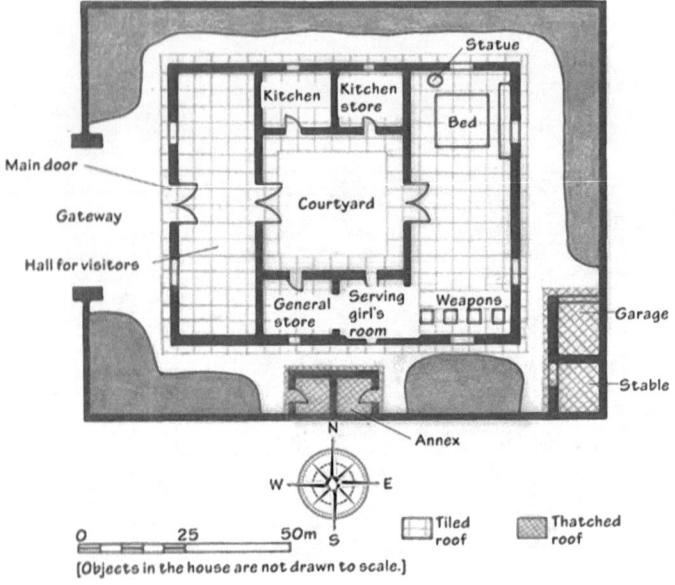

Labels on plan: Statue, Kitchen, Kitchen store, Bed, Main door, Gateway, Courtyard, Hall for visitors, General store, Serving girl's room, Weapons, Garage, Stable, Annex, N, W, E, S

Tiled roof / Thatched roof

0 25 50m

[Objects in the house are not drawn to scale.]

Plan of Brahmdutt's House

that she had no motive. In the absence of a will, it was hard to say who had one, but very clearly, unless Brahmdutt had tortured her, she had the most to lose from a change of master, a change that would put her in a position of uncertainty.

I thought about the reclining position of the corpse as the three of them had described it. Was he asleep? He definitely did not have a warning of the attack, as his hands were not damaged as they would have been if he had raised them to ward off the blows.

I put all of this together with Virsa's scenarios, and there was only one conclusion if I rejected the possibility of some divine magic—the one Meghnath's report would confirm or refute. I sensed the serving girl watching me from the bedroom window. Suddenly, I wanted to be home in Vrushali's arms. Something told me they would be open for me. I walked to the open main door and stepped in. The girl came to the door which opened into the courtyard. I stepped to the side so that she would not have the light behind her. We stood facing each other.

'Who else works for the household? I am sure there are others I have not met.'

'Yes, King. There is a cook, a man who comes twice a day. Early morning and late afternoon. Then there is cleaner, a woman. A gardener too. He also manages the stable.'

I had planned to talk to each of the workers, but by then I was quite sure they were all irrelevant. I fingered my earlobe.

'Perhaps you do not know, there are limited ways for you to get freedom. It can happen by a decree, or you have to buy it. It does not happen by promise.' I tried to be gentle.

Her face clouded.

'Is there anything you want to tell me?' I asked. Now her face fell, and I felt sorry for her.

'Many people have asked me for things. I try not to disappoint them. You know about me.'

She nodded but kept silent. I knew it would not be easy for her, this girl who had lived in a caged world. I turned and walked toward my chariot. Again, I felt her gaze on me, and I knew she would need help. I made a note to take care of her later, when all this was finished.

The charioteer was half-asleep, and he woke up with a start when the chariot lurched. I sometimes wondered how my father had survived this job for all his life. A large part of the job seemed to consist of doing nothing. It was true: as Virsa had once told me, your parents and teachers are the only ones in this world who want you to do better than them. And when you have done better, you are sometimes—at least in your thoughts—less than respectful toward them.

I was itching to get home, but I thought I might as well try my luck at the secret service building first. Perhaps Officer Meghnath had some news for me. I told the charioteer to drive there.

On the way, we drove through the street where we had encountered the homeless. We had to drive slowly, as it was humming with life now. The people still waved to me, and some of them cheered me. It felt good. Soon there were three children running behind the chariot. I looked over my shoulder. The frontrunner was sweating, and his hair swayed from side to side as he ran bare feet. His eyes were wide with excitement and exertion, and his mouth was wide open as he panted for air. As we got closer to the royal avenue, the road became less congested, and we pulled ahead of the runners. I turned around, groped for the coins in my purse, and threw one each to the runners. Two of them caught the coins, and the third one got his after rummaging for it while the other two laughed at him. One of them cupped his mouth and put all his lung power into a shout, but I could not read his lips. We turned on to the royal avenue.

The sound which followed was jarring, because it came from a grown man. I turned back again and realised that it was Duryodhan shouting from his chariot, which was behind us. We slowed down and stopped, and Duryodhan jumped off his chariot when he got close. I got off and faced him.

'Brother!' He shouted again. He had his arms outstretched, and he had a very serious look. We stood there for a while, facing each other. I should have responded, but I was frozen. He took a step forward, went down on his knees and joined his palms. Then he stood up, walked to me and crushed me in an embrace. I felt as if time had frozen. I could feel the stares of a hundred people on us.

'I tried to find you!' Duryodhan spoke into my ear. 'You had disappeared. Look, I was wrong. You know I get impatient and frustrated. You know how I am. I told you it's very hard to make friends after a certain age, and I really don't want to lose you.'

I could only nod. He held on to my left shoulder, and his grip tightened.

'Come to the palace. I want to talk to you. Or are you going home? I will not stop you.'

'Brother,' I said in a husky voice, 'I have to go home. And perhaps to stop by at the secret service building. About that case, you know, I think it is the same old things—'

'Tell me about it later, Brother,' he said. 'Yes, I expect it will be the same old things. I realised I was not being smart, apart from asking you to do wrong. The only way to avoid war, really, is for Yudhishthir to give up his claim on the throne. Or for me to do so.'

This world, the only one of the three worlds that I had seen, was big enough, I thought. We had not seen its ends. And the country, this land, had enough for everyone. But we wanted more. More land, more tribute, more women, more horses, more chariots, more elephants, more cattle. Yes, there would be a war.

'I know you won't tell me what you are thinking.' Duryodhan chuckled.

'Nothing much.' I shrugged.

'If you were thinking that there is no relationship without a motive, as your guru taught you, it is true. I will need you in the war, but that is not the point. The point is I need you by my side before it.' He looked away from me for an instant and looked straight into my eyes.

'Do you sometimes think that I am using you?' he asked, very softly.

The people in the street had made way for us, and they could not hear us. The charioteers could, though they stood with their heads lowered, pretending they had disappeared.

'Brother, I was nothing without you,' I said. 'On that day, when I challenged Arjun, they would have crushed me—'

'On that day, I did myself a favour.' Duryodhan cut me short and smiled back at me. 'Now go home. I need to talk to you tomorrow.' He turned serious and walked back toward his chariot. He allowed his charioteer to help him up. He made that sign of his, with his fist clenched and arm raised, and he grinned at me. I saluted him. His chariot turned around and receded into the distance. He turned around twice to make the sign, and I responded with salutes.

I leaned against the pole while the chariot moved toward the secret service building. I felt too embarrassed to look at the awestruck people around me. The charioteer had looked at me as if I were a god.

Officer Meghnath was waiting for me at the turn of the road which led to the headquarters. He must have known I was headed that way.

I gestured to him to get on to the chariot. He climbed on and signalled that we should not start. He whispered the few words which told me all I needed to know: 'It is true, what you suspected about the homeless man.'

It did not matter very much if someone heard him. I nodded, clasped his shoulder and thanked him. He saluted with an extra-deferential namaste and jumped off.

It was time to report to Shri Vidur. I told the charioteer to turn back toward the palace. He looked at me in surprise before turning back. I caught a distant glimpse of the street which led to my mansion and then it receded out of view.

VI

THE ROOM OVERLOOKED a compound with a small pool full of lotus flowers. A single blue lotus stood out in the middle of all the others, which were white. A guard had escorted me there when I sent word that I wanted to see Shri Vidur. I kept myself busy looking at the iridescent play of light on the surface of the pool, thinking through the way I would present the facts of the case.

I heard Shri Vidur's precise footsteps approaching the room well before he strode in. The court was in session, and he looked a bit flustered. He smiled cursorily, and asked, 'So, King Anga, all is well?'

'All is well, Sir.'

'What news of the case?'

'The case is solved, Sir,' I said.

He did not show surprise, but he did raise his eyebrows. 'Are you sure?' I shrugged.

'Tell me.'

'First of all, Duryodhan's involvement in the case is extraneous. He went to see Brahmdutt, he was upset about Brahmdutt's view on the ascension issue, but Brahmdutt was seen accompanying Duryodhan out of the door of his house and returning unscathed.

"Then, there is the involvement of Bheem. According to secret service reports, Bheem was seen talking to the sentry who patrolled that street, and the sentry was seen to suddenly have extra money to spend."

Vidur frowned. "Are you suggesting that Bheem is—"

I raised my hand and he stopped. "I am saying what I said. I believe that incident has no bearing on the murder."

"That's good to know," Vidur said. "So, do you have a view on who murdered Brahmdutt? This then becomes a much less politically loaded question, but it is still important."

"Yes, I do. To begin, allow me to report the facts relevant to the murder: Brahmdutt has been pilfering a part of the tribute that flows from Kushasthali to Hastinapur. The records of transmissions from Kushasthali to Hastinapur, and those of receipts at Hastinapur do not match. The secret service had found this. The next steps would have been for them to tell you, and for you to bring this matter to Shri Balaram's notice."

Vidur smacked his head. "What a fool! With a job like his, with no dependents, it's really pathetic. Is this information from the secret service?"

"Yes, I have made good use of their network, and they were extremely helpful. After some persuasion."

"I have heard about a desk in their headquarters being broken," he said with a smile.

"I promised to get it replaced," I said.

"Yes, of course. So, who killed Brahmdutt?" he asked. A lesser person would have betrayed some signs of impatience. Not Shri Vidur. From his tone, you might have thought he was asking me if I had had lunch.

"The answer comes," I said, "from motive in this case, apart from the facts of the incident. Who has gained?"

I waited for him to answer me. He held my gaze, and then signalled with his hand that I should keep going. A flicker of a smile lit his face.

"It was Brahmdutt himself," I said. Vidur frowned now. I went on, "He had money—it is hard to say how much, but it must be more than enough to last a few lifetimes. He was about to get exposed, and though it is hard to say for sure, he might have sensed it. For example, he might have known that the records of transmission and receipt of funds were being investigated."

"What does the victim's motive have to do with it? This can't be a suicide?" Vidur asked.

"I could give you a long-winded answer, but this is the simple truth," I said. "Brahmdutt had six toes on each foot, and that gave him an idea. He knew that if he just absconded, there would be a search for him and there was a risk of his being caught. He saw a homeless man with six toes on each foot and a build similar to his own. On the day of the murder—not his murder—he brought the chariot right up to the door of his house. The homeless man was in it. How he got him onto it without others noticing, I do not know at all."

"Did you try to find out?" Vidur asked with a raised eyebrow.

"No, Sir, I didn't," I said. The poor homeless man must have been asked to take a bath, and perhaps to wait to be served by the serving girl, Amba, who is quite a beauty. He must have been beside himself! While he lay on the bed, Brahmdutt first stabbed him and then bludgeoned his face with a mace. It is not clear to me how Brahmdutt hid himself—but most probably he hid behind the head of the bed, and it was already dark.' Vidur frowned, but stayed quiet.

'When the deed was done, he must have slipped below the bed with the weapons, taking care not to disturb the patterns of the blood. When the sentry and Amba came in, Amba collapsed.'

Vidur had closed his eyes, and he seemed half asleep as he stood there. I found myself warming up to this wise, ugly man who worked himself to exhaustion, but I did not know whether to continue.

He opened one eye first, and then the other one. 'You were saying, about the girl, that she collapsed, is that right?'

'This girl Amba, yes,' I continued, speaking a bit faster now. 'She probably did not have to put on an act when she collapsed. The sentry had to go for help. Brahmdutt had enough time to wipe the weapons, and to take them and the cloth with which he wiped them, and his loot, and lower himself out of the rear window onto the grass below. He must have gone across the garden, jumped the wall, crossed the embankment and got into a waiting boat. It must have been a bit difficult with all those weapons and the bundle, but it was not impossible. He would need the weapons anyway. He would also have had to schedule his getting into the boat just after the river patrol left.'

I followed Vidur's gaze to the lotus pool and to the blue lotus. The light had softened, and its blue had become more radiant. I was tempted to wade into the pool and pluck it for Vrushali. I wondered where the thought came from. I noticed with a start that Vidur was looking at me with a smile.

'You could take it,' he said with a deadpan face, 'but you would look silly carrying it on Royal Avenue.'

I had to hang my head, and then to figure out where I should continue from. 'That's right. As I was saying, that was how Brahmdutt got away, I think. Amba only had to lock the window behind him and get back to the position she was in. Also, before the murder, Brahmdutt did one more thing to confound the investigation. He created a bogey by going to the priest at the ghat and asking that, of all people, I cremate him, as he has no son.'

'He mentioned you by name?' Vidur was doubtful.

'Yes. Of course, he could not have known about my being asked to investigate the case.'

Vidur walked slowly to the window and gazed at the lotus pool. 'I think ...,' he stopped. He interlocked his hands behind him and stretched. 'Look at your analysis,' he said. 'You say this must have happened, that might have happened, and probably here is how it happened. Where is the proof?'

'There is no proof, Sir, and there will not be,' I replied. 'But there are some facts: Brahmdutt is said to have been murdered. He is a member of society, and his disappearance counts. But there is another man with six toes on each foot, with a similar build, who is also missing! This man did not exist for us, but the secret service has verified that at least some men for whom he did exist state that he is missing. And the room of the murder is indeed a closed room. I have verified that myself. There is no other way this murder could have happened. There is no alternative!'

Vidur looked thoughtful. 'What did Brahmdutt gain by all this?' He stopped for a while and then answered the question himself. 'If you had not come up with this explanation, he would have lived happily ever after. Even now, he might still, given that he has had a clear start on us, and we do not know how successful a manhunt will be. But I will launch one … let me think this through.' He closed his eyes and traced the lines on his forehead with his fingers.

'Tell me, have you thought about the element of chance in your explanation? You met a group of homeless men, they said something about a missing person. The missing man turned out to be the victim. Isn't it hard to believe? I am not saying I don't believe you, but do you believe it works like this?'

'It is hard to believe, Sir,' I replied, 'but this is how it happened. Brahmdutt created an impossible crime, but I got lucky and solved it.'

'And what if the serving girl had brought two men in?' He asked.

I do not think that my mind went blank, but I have to confess that it froze for an instant, like a deer surprised by a hunter. I pictured the sky as I had seen it when I was up on the cliff in the morning: pristine, blue. I was so sure then that I had it all worked out.

I felt Vidur's hand on my shoulder. 'Don't look so crushed,' he said. 'At that time of the night, with the sentries being far apart… No, I think Brahmdutt had worked it out. He could count on only one man being there at first.'

Vidur smiled. He looked at the pool for some time. 'It makes sense. Tell me only this, how did you reach your conclusion? What triggered the thought?'

'To be honest, Sir, it was a discussion with someone else,' I said. 'He listed many possibilities, and one possibility, the chance that the victim was not really who we thought he was, seemed to be the one plausible explanation.'

'Right, I think that's clear. My mind is all clogged up, now, with the affairs of the court. I wish I had more time to think this through. Tell me, out of the possibilities, this one was the one plausible one. But what if there are other possibilities?' He paused for a moment. 'Actually, no. The case of the missing homeless man cannot be a coincidence. I wonder how Brahmdutt got him to come home? He could have enticed him with money or with the girl, of course, but what made the man foolish enough to believe him?'

'We will never know, Sir.'

'No, no. I will know. If only I have time, but first, it's most important to try to get Brahmdutt if we can. He will have made sure the girl knows nothing of his whereabouts. There is a lot we won't know, but I am satisfied with what we have got. The important thing was for Shri Balaram to be convinced that we did everything we could. Now we will also have to demonstrate that we have been diligent in trying to track Brahmdutt.'

'I have two requests, Sir,' I said.

'Of course, speak freely,' Vidur said.

'First, about an officer in the secret service, Meghnath. I found him quite exceptional and fast in his work. I would like for him to be commended,' I said. 'Second, the girl Amba. She is an accomplice to murder, yes, but perhaps she can be forgiven and freed? I can ask my wife to take her into service.'

'Well, about this Meghnath, I am not sure people should be commended for just doing their jobs,' Vidur mused. 'I'll think about it. About that girl, I think it will be very hard for her. It's like I told you, I cannot be seen to be soft on a slave girl because my mother was a slave. Are you interested in her?' He asked.

The look on my face must have conveyed my alarm to him.

He said, 'No, you are not the type to acquire women. Like me.' He smiled, and I was relieved that he had no idea how fickle she had exposed my mind to be.

'I think she was promised freedom by Brahmdutt. I have not interrogated her, but he must have promised to send money to her later, so that she could buy her freedom.'

'Must have, again,' said Vidur.

'I could find out,' I said.

'Yes, you could, but I think we will have to arrest her. She will suffer, and that homeless man has suffered. I have my doubts about whether we will catch Brahmdutt. It is not a perfect world.' He laid a hand on my shoulder. 'You have done a fair job. You have done me proud. I will … at least say that I am very satisfied with the outcome.' He broke into a broad grin. It transformed his face.

'I will leave, Sir.'

'May the Sun God be with you,' he said, sincerely.

I bowed and did a namaste. When I looked up, he was bathed in the golden light reflected from the pool. He grinned again, and I smiled back at him.

The energy I had felt coursing through my veins in the morning seemed to have dissipated as I walked out. I was satisfied with my work, but Vidur's words about the world being imperfect kept running through my mind.

I let the charioteer help me step up on to the chariot. The ride back home was short. The sun had started to plummet, and it was twilight when I reached my mansion. The lamps were lit, and Vrushali was waiting for me at the door. I stepped down without aid and ran toward her. She embraced me, and when I held her I felt tears on her cheeks. I felt an animal urge to take her inside quickly, and tip her over onto our bed, but when I laid my hand on her fluttering heart and looked closer at her in that soft light, I sensed that she had not eaten or slept well since I left.

'If we had to go, I would have gone with you,' she murmured.

'I know,' I said, and I caressed her back. 'I want to eat with you first.'

She smiled through her tears.

We had a quick meal of fruit, and then I took her by her hand to the sleeping room. She was exhausted. I gave her a hug and lowered her to the bed. I started to pat her to sleep. Usually she was the one who did this for me.

'Are you sure?'

'That I will let you sleep?' I whispered. 'Yes.'

She smiled with her eyes closed. 'Do you think there will be a big war?'

I thought about it. At this rate, yes, there would be a war. It would be bloody. But it might be many years from now. We did not know which side would win. The winners would record these times as they liked.

'There might be,' I said. 'What it means is that we should enjoy what we have, because it will not last.'

'I hear so much praise of you that it makes me very happy,' she said. 'What makes you do the things you do?' She was mumbling now.

I looked at the rise and fall of her breasts for some time. 'They taunted me so often,' I said. 'I had so many names: Vasusena, Radheya.' I patted her gently. 'In the forest for some time they called me the man with no name. Then they settled on this name, Karn, because of my ears.' I fingered my earlobe.

'I want to live my life in a way that will inspire many parents to name their sons after me.' I was surprised I had admitted it. I looked at her to see if she found it funny.

She was breathing deeply. She had not heard me. I enjoyed looking at her for a long time while I waited for sleep to come to me.

The Meeting

KRISHNA, ONE OF the avatars of Vishnu, straddles the narrative of the *Mahabharat*. He influences many of its key turning points. On the first day of the great war, when Arjun did not find himself up to the task of fighting his seniors and his kin, it was Krishna who delivered a sermon to energise the despondent Arjun and remind him of his duty. The philosophical discussion between Krishna and Arjun forms the sacred text *Bhagavad Gita*.

Krishna's life was threatened even before his birth. The evil Kamsa deposed his own father, Ugrasen, and usurped the throne of Mathura. Kamsa was fearful of a curse that predicted that he would be killed by his sister Devaki's eighth son. He imprisoned Devaki and her husband Vasudev and killed their first six sons. The seventh survived; though Kamsa thought Devaki had miscarried the eighth son, she had in fact transferred the foetus to Vasudev's other wife. Krishna was the eighth son. Before Kamsa could kill him, he was smuggled out of the prison cell and sent to Gokul village, where he was brought up by his foster parents, the cowherd, Nand, and his wife, Yashodha.

As a child, Krishna subdued the fearsome snake king, Kalia, and danced on its multiple hoods. Kamsa sent a witch to kill Krishna. The witch smeared her nipple with poison and breast-fed him, but Krishna survived, and the witch died. Krishna survived several such murder attempts and went on to slay Kamsa and reinstall Ugrasen on the throne of Mathura. Thus, Krishna destroyed evil and restored good.

Krishna has inspired many historical figures including the saint Chaitanya, the poet Surdas, the mystic and poetess Meerabai and the Muslim statesman-poet Abdul Rahim Khane-Khana. Krishna remains a dominant figure in present Hindu thought. The many facets of his life are common in calendar art images. These include Krishna as the cute boy butter thief, virile lover, enchanting flute player and the preacher of the *Bhagavad Gita.* His birthday celebration is a major festival, Krishna Janmashtami, and he is an important figure in other festivals including Holi and Rath Yatra. Krishna represents the ideal of the saviour who smashes class barriers and delivers humanity from evil.

◆ • • ◆

I

 HERE ARE THINGS *a man will do, and things a man will not do. What will I do today? Will I point a gun at an unarmed man, my chief, a man who saved my life, and pull the trigger?*

Wang Xiaobo readied himself to stop thinking. That was good, that he could will himself to. He prepared to censor his thoughts and switched his thought phone on. It had taken him a long time to get used to the bloody thing and its weird premise that projecting one's thoughts simplified communication.

He had changed taxis twice from the railway station, as usual. Now the gray, unwelcoming building stood across the road. It had been a long journey from the mild coolness of Delhi to this chilly morning in Pudong. He had chosen to take the maglev train through Lhasa instead of the shuttle from Delhi. The charm of the shuttle had worn off when he was in his sixties. Now he hated cattle class travel. On the train, they had played the *Yellow River Concerto* a little too often, for the benefit of the tourists, but he could live with that. The food was bland and the wine cheap. One of the hostesses was expensive and delicious. There were no surprises. He had slept well in his private sleeper cabin. Forty years ago, at the midpoint of his life, he would have laughed if someone told him that he would be able to enjoy a drink, a meal and a girl in the year 2049.

It felt good to be back, after—what was it, a few years more than a decade? After Li Yinhe left him, three decades ago, he hadn't wanted to ever come back. Now that he was here, he loved the sameness, the feeling of belonging. He loved the frost that formed as he breathed out. A craving for a nicotine patch nagged at him, but he knew it was too close to the moment of truth.

He had worn a short Indian kurta which would hang loosely over the gun. The fibreglass Laser QSZ40, his weapon of choice, should have been weightless, but it had a weight, nonetheless. The project review meeting would be troublesome. Though he had got his assistant Chen Qingyang to do a dry run, he was worried about how he would cope with the stress of the meeting while preoccupied by the idea of killing Luo Xiaosi. *I should get a move on, shouldn't be seen hanging around here*, he thought. An elderly woman in a Mandarin dress turned her head toward him, hoping to hear more. He made an effort to blank his mind, and she kept going.

Move on! The light turned green, and he walked on. He was there in front of the HCBB head office. It was fourteen years since he had walked past the grilled gate. Not much had changed in the exterior of that little gray building. The guard camera probably had faster recognition software. The red dots on the display formed a message: 'Welcome, Wang Xiaobo.' There was no one else around, which meant that he would be the last one to get in for the Programme Review. That was okay by him. He took a deep breath and enjoyed the nip in the air.

He walked past the lawn, controlling his breath. *Fresh grass has that smell. Why isn't there a word for it in Mandarin or Hindi? Or English. The language I picked up last, and the one we spoke most often.*

He placed both thumbs on the Checkpad, and the glass panes parted. The reception was bare. No pictures, no signs. Just an ornate desk right in front, and the closed door to the meeting room number one on the left.

The girl at the desk took his breath away. Wide eyes, high cheekbones, uncoloured black hair. *She must be, what, thirty? What is it about her? And what is it about me?* Luckily she was too far away to hear him yet. He had thought that after the thousandth woman he would get over it, marginal utility and all that. But he hadn't. He gave her his best smile.

She wore a black business suit. It hid her curves, but he could make out the beginnings of the swell of a glorious bust.

Region Head Wang Xiaobo, from Delhi office.

They're waiting. She smiled a strained smile.

He tilted his head. *You're incredibly sexy.*

I know. She gazed back at him.

I only have a few hours here, and it's been a long time since I had a Chinese woman.

She laughed. *You should stay longer.* Her voice, at least the way the thought phone relayed it, was silky smooth.

I wish I could. Is a quick one really out of the question?

I'm afraid so. You're too old and ugly. She blushed.

I'm only eighty. You look wonderful when you blush. His gaze fell to that glorious bust of hers. *Are they real?*

She rolled her eyes. *Yes, of course.*

They're magnificent. My congratulations.

My boyfriend loves them. You should move on, no? The meeting's due to start.

Ah, well. I guess I'll end up playing with myself later.

Up to you. Don't strain yourself too much.

He laughed. *Does Project Head Luo Xiaosi get lucky with you?*

Her eyes flashed. *No. Are you carrying any weapons?*

He looked into her eyes and smiled. *No.* Without a pause: *I guess I should go on?*

Yes, you should. And find someone to live with.

It's not as easy for me as it is for you, he thought. She laughed. *You have a wonderful laugh.*

Thank you.

Take care.

You too, Sir.

Wang Xiaobo felt an unusual pang of regret, a fleeting discomfort that a line of propriety had been crossed and it shouldn't have been. He had also crossed the barrier. It felt unreal. 'You will see,' he had been briefed, 'depending on technology creates openings for the enemy.' It had taken months of training and repeating the kriya till he could master the art of controlling his thoughts only once, for five seconds. It took him an hour to do it again one more time, but after that he needed days to repeat the masking of thought.

If it wasn't for thought phones, there would have been detectors and guards instead of just the question, 'Are you carrying any weapons?'

He walked toward the entrance. Once he was out of her hearing range, he felt the urge to exhale, but he resisted. He walked on toward the meeting room. He looked into the detector on the right of the door, and it swung open. He walked in.

II

THEY WERE ALL in the room, waiting for him. Luo Xiaosi sat at the head of the table, in his trademark white shirt, with his hands folded. He and Wang Xiaobo had not spoken on personal terms since Li Yinhe left him.

Did it have to be that way? His thoughts were drowned in the cacophony of the group.

Hey Boss, welcome, you look good. That would be his assistant, Chen Qingyang, who would be presenting first today. She looked good, too, in a business suit.

You've become half-Indian. You were almost late. The Brazil office head, in an expensive-looking shirt with cufflinks smiled at Wang Xiaobo.

Ah, Tripitaka himself ... we've been losing there but you haven't lost your swagger, ha ha. His rival, Ah Lan, the Russia man. He looked every bit the Krav Maga specialist that he was, no less so now that his hair was all white.

The other thoughts got drowned in the general melee. Luo Xiaosi brought his hand down. *Quiet please.* There was a silence. *Wang Xiaobo and his team will start now by sharing the background with us, for the benefit of some of the younger team members.*

Hey, Wang Xiaobo, you shared a lot with the Chief, no? That had to be Ah Lan again. Luo Xiaosi stared him down.

Thought phones off. Luo Xiaosi said, reaching behind his ear with his left hand. Everyone followed suit. Wang Xiaobo still found it eerie, this first moment of silence between the closing of thought and opening of verbal communication.

Luo Xiaosi cleared his throat and said, 'Meeting starts now. Rules apply.' He paused. 'I guess you all need to clear your throats. It's a sign of the times, isn't it?'

There was the usual round of polite throat clearing sounds.

Chen Qingyang stood up. Wang Xiaobo could see that she was a little awed to be presenting to this audience, but he knew it would be okay. He was quite comfortable with the choice he had made. She looked at him, and he gave her a nod.

She touched the F64 button and projected her notebook. The first hologram formed in the air above the table. It showed the Taj Mahal below the Great Wall. The graphic title read: 'HCBB Project, 2009—2089: Harmonisation of India's Long-Term Development. Midpoint Review, 15 August 2049.'

'As Region Head Wang Xiaobo has advised,' Chen Qingyang said, 'I will first brief you on the background which lead to the formation of the HCBB Project in 2009. Next, I will summarise the components of HCBB. This is being done for the benefit of the younger members of the group.' Her voice came out a bit strained, but Wang Xiaobo knew that would be overlooked. It was natural. 'I will then move to the achievements by 2029, which I saw firsthand. Finally, Wang Xiaobo will take the section on the current crisis which has brought us here, and we will seek consensus on the way forward.'

Luo Xiaosi nodded a couple of times.

'As always, the graphics are just to aid the discussion.' She paused and smiled. 'And to give business to Lenosoft.'

There was a round of polite laughter.

'Please do not hesitate to interrupt me or correct me, especially when it comes to my presentation of the background information.'

Luo Xiaosi nodded in approval, as Wang Xiaobo knew he would.

'To begin at the beginning,' Chen Qingyang continued, 'in 2009, there was a real possibility that India could become a developed country if sense prevailed.' She clicked the remote. 'This graphic shows the GDP growth of the country since the year 1900. As you see, the per capita income before independence grew at less than 2%. After independence, the GDP grew, but the death rate decreased as well. For some decades, these two benefits cancelled each other out. After that, a steady, irrevocable growth pattern emerged in the mid-1980s. By 2009, the growth looked spectacular.'

Ah Lan leaned forward, all concentration.

'I understand that Luo Xiaosi and Wang Xiaobo made personal visits to India and came away impressed with India's potential and relieved at their bottlenecks.' Wang Xiaobo looked at Luo Xiaosi. He sat with his elbows on the table, fingers joined, and chin resting on both thumbs.

'To help harmonise India's development while minimising its impact on China's peaceful existence, these two gentlemen formulated the HCBB project.

HCBB does not have a full form now, but I understand that back then, the idea was that, in the event of detection, the acronym could stand for High Capacity Broadband.'

Wang Xiaobo raised his hand. Chen Qingyang nodded for him to speak.

'Well, we never discussed this,' he said, 'but it was also a play on the phrase "Hindi Chini Bhai Bhai," which one of the many idiot Indian leaders, an Allahabadi who didn't know Hindi, dreamt up a long time back.'

There were a few titters, but more blank looks. 'What does that mean?' Ah Lan asked.

'The phrase? It means, "Indians and Chinese are brothers,"' replied Wang Xiaobo.

'That's what some of our idiot leaders say as well,' Ah Lan shot back. 'That's why we're clandestine even within the Sixth Bureau, right?'

'Whatever,' Wang Xiaobo said.

Luo Xiaosi cleared his throat. 'Can we move on please? Chen Qingyang,' he smiled at her, 'can you summarise this section quickly?'

'Sure,' Chen Qingyang shrugged. 'Well, in summary, there was a danger of India achieving solid growth, but there were mitigating factors. These may be summarised under the categories of defence, government, health, education, business, media, internal security and others.'

She's warming up now, Wang Xiaobo thought. *Her delivery is smoother.*

'Firstly, their arms production capabilities. Their newspapers went on and on about their superpower status, but they couldn't make weapons for nuts. Their R&D was sabotaged by leaders who wanted bribes for buying weapons from all over. They had long-running projects like these.'

She skipped two graphics and stopped at a graphic showing pictures of a helicopter, a fighter aircraft and a tank. The bulleted text stated: 'As of 2009, Advanced Light Helicopter, Dhruv: light but not much of a helicopter, definitely not advanced. Main Battle Tank, Arjun: couldn't do battle till thirty years after its planned launch. Light Combat Aircraft, Tejas: light, could just about fly, but useless for combat.'

There was laughter all around.

'It is interesting that according to our estimates, even in those days, the borders were not well guarded, and at some points it was possible to bribe the border guards to take trucks into India, not to mention a few hundred people.'

Ah Lan looked like he was about to raise his hand, but he changed his mind.

'Next, government. Even in 2009, though both China and India were corrupt, it was easier to get Indian leaders to act against their national interest. And the Indians were already taking bribes to follow the rules, unlike some of our black sheep who took bribes to break the rules.' The graphic showed an exponential curve. 'As you can see here,' Chen Qingyang continued, 'on the X axis, you have the timeline, on the Y axis the segment (politicians, police, judges and so on). The Z axis gives the estimated amount of black money smuggled into secret bank accounts. The cumulative value by 2009 was already equal to five years GDP, which was quite an achievement.'

The team was silent. Chen Qingyang had told him the team would find a 3D graph hard to digest, but Wang Xiaobo had overruled her. He believed there should be a few hard graphics in every review meeting.

'Continuing to health, you see two pictures in this graphic.' The graphic showed two hospital wards, one completely decrepit and the other a swanky new building. 'One is a general ward of the LagGaiJung Hospital in Delhi, which is self-explanatory. The new building is a mall in a so-called cyber city. This mall, with one hundred thousand feet of retail space, came up without a sewage connection. You can imagine the possibilities for long-term health impact that such projects created.'

There were murmurs of approval.

Chen Qingyang skipped two more graphics. The one she stopped at showed a rundown building half-covered with bulging sacks. 'Coming now to education: by 2009, we see that forty percent of Indian children did not have access to a school. This picture is of a government school in the state of Bihar. It was actually counted as a school but was being used as a storage area for the headmaster's rice crop.'

Ah Lan burst into laughter.

'The Indian media, which we shall come to, went gaga about the IITs and how well they were rated by the Americans, but luckily for us most IIT graduates went on to earn MBAs. Two years of discussing cases like Southwest Airlines and Starbucks idiotized them and left them fit to become bankers or consultants.' Luo Xiaosi did a thumbs up, and she smiled. 'Luckily, the Indian government had already decided to invest in more IITs, the logic being that you should have more of a good thing. On the other hand, there was only one medical equivalent of the IITs in the country.' She flicked the button, and the graphic showed rows of trendy-looking young men and women wearing headphones. She looked at Luo Xiaosi and waited for him to nod approval.

'In this graphic, you see a call centre employee. These people took a lot of pride in doing B-grade work farmed out to them by Western companies. The Indian media called these B-grade workers knowledge workers and wrote that India was becoming a knowledge superpower. Moving on, you'll see some examples of how great intellectuals helped to make an idiot nation of the country.' She moved to a graphic which showed a book cover with a bald, bearded man next to it.

'Here you see a book by the great intellectual, Doctor Freemind. The book is called *The World is Free*. The good doctor did research by talking to the CEOs of body shopping firms which called themselves IT companies. He helped us greatly by writing that if Americans weren't careful, their children wouldn't get to eat as Indian children would take away their livelihoods. The Indian journalists loved it and ignored, for example,'—she flicked the remote and the graphic changed to an official-looking report—'this report describing the trafficking of children in India.'

Wang Xiaobo leaned back. *It's going well so far. But the hard part will start soon. And after that? Will I be ready?* He interlocked his fingers behind his back, and then traced the outline of the gun tucked away in the small of his back.

'Equally helpful was the role of management education. Unlike us, the Indians loved the clerical professions and had already started to ignore useful kinds of education. If I may skip some holograms… Yes, here you see a photo of the very intelligent--looking Indian management guru, Doctor PK Sehlade, who wrote that the Johnny Lever company was helping the people at the Base of Poverty by selling skin whitening creams to them. In fact, the management journals of the world were flooded with Indian gurus writing seminal articles every month, and no one smelled the stink.'

Someone sniggered loudly. Wang Xiaobo noticed with approval that Chen Qingyang had an eye on Luo Xiaosi most of the time, though she engaged with all of them. He made the rotating sign with his finger, signalling her to move faster.

Chen Qingyang nodded and continued: 'Though we have more material available for later perusal, I think I will summarise quickly now, and request additional comments from Luo Xiaosi and Wang Xiaobo at the end.' She looked again at Luo Xiaosi and then turned to Wang Xiaobo. 'A few points should suffice. Firstly, in spite of the tremendous growth, there were no branded Indian products being used in the First World, which then excluded China. Secondly, the Indian love for a game called cricket, in which people stand still ninety percent of the time, combined with the fact that sports development was done by the government, ensured that they won one or two medals in every Olympics. Thirdly, while they complimented themselves on their Bollywood films, most of the world found them too embarrassing to watch. Some of them were good, but as for the average film, you will see some subtitled trailers in the appendices.' The audience leaned forward, except for Ah Lan, who stretched and yawned.

'They show, for example, how the good Malhotras, who have houses in London and whose handsome boys travel by helicopter and are attended to by white servants, triumph over the evil Saxenas, after doing dance numbers with long-haired blondes pirouetting in the background. On internal security, there were fairly satisfactory developments in the form of the so-called Islamic terrorists from the Western front of India. Additionally, about one third of the country was commandeered by the Naxalite rebels while the journalists went on and on about the ISI menace.' She closed the notebook and gestured toward Luo Xiaosi.

'I now ask Luo Xiaosi and Wang Xiaobo to add on to this summary, and then I will explain the components of the HCBB project.'

The room was quiet. Then Luo Xiaosi spoke softly: 'I think most aspects have been covered well. There were all of these encouraging signs, yes, but there were also underlying strengths which needed to be neutralised.' Luo Xiaosi's shirt had taken on a light-blue hue in the reflected light of the blank hologram.

Wang Xiaobo looked at the others, who were hanging on to every word. *You've got to hand it to him, he's a born leader.*

'Remember,' Luo Xiaosi continued, 'there was a fairly decent industrial base, some achievements in aerospace and nuclear areas where there was no option of importing equipment and getting bribes, and so on. By the way, the average life expectancy at independence in 1947, after two hundred years of plunder by the British, was forty years. One of the largest ever movements of people out of poverty anywhere had also taken place from 1989 to 2009.' He looked at Chen Quingyang, who nodded.

'I would like to dwell on the doctrine aspects. As I always say, patriotism, discipline, doctrine, pragmatism: these are the four pillars for our work. We have dealt with corruption as well, like the case last year...' Luo Xiaosi shrugged and sighed. Wang Xiaobo recalled that Luo Xiaosi had killed Le Du for treason in this very room, as a lesson for the rest of them. The news had travelled fast to Delhi. 'Anyway, we continue to work, and we take commitment to these four pillars as a minimum requirement.' He rubbed his fingernails against each other as he said this.

It's a long time since I saw anyone do that thing with the fingernails, Wang Xiaobo thought.

'What was our theory? First of all, moral influence is what causes people to be in harmony with their leaders in life and death. We decided that we must weaken their moral influence and base our efforts on deception. There was no deception worth the name in the Naxalite project. As I hope you know, we must feign incapacity when capable and inactivity when active; when we were near, we must make it appear that we were far away. We must anger and confuse their generals, divide their people when they are united and—above all—pretend inferiority and encourage arrogance.' The group listened with rapt attention.

'Are there any questions?'

There wouldn't be. All of the elders owed their lives to Luo Xiaosi. For the younger members, it was enough to be in the same room with him.

'On a lighter note,' Luo Xiaosi said, 'I would like to add that my heart really leapt up every time I went to Mumbai. Those guys went on and on about how it was the Shanghai or New York of India. Actually, even then, it was the shit and racism capital of the world.'

The room exploded into laughter.

'Anyway, Wang Xiaobo and Chen Qingyang, now that we have set up the background, let's look at HCBB as it was originally framed.'

Wang Xiaobo gestured toward Chen Qingyang, and she stood and flicked to a new hologram.

III

THE HOLOGRAM THIS time, for the first time, was a series of words: 'To win one hundred victories in one hundred battles is not the acme of skill. To subdue the enemy without fighting is the acme of skill.'

Chen Qingyang started to speak. 'I understand that Luo Xiaosi and Wang Xiaobo framed HCBB based on major building blocks supported by the four pillars.' She flicked to the next hologram. It showed a crowd of jostling demonstrators who had their hands raised and seemed to be shouting.

'Firstly, there is the matter of ... words. As we are taught, what does Heaven ever say? Yet there are the four seasons going round and there are the hundred things coming into being. On the other hand, a love for words, debates and essays was deeply ingrained into the Indian psyche. This reinforced a natural tendency to shirk work, especially in the intelligentsia. This was seen as a great advantage for us to maintain.' She paused to take a sip of water.

'Secondly, again as we all have studied, for a nation to prosper, Heaven must smile on it, the Earth must be favourable to it and the people must be at peace. And to be at peace, the nation must have enough arms and enough food, and the government must have the trust of the common people. So to prevent a nation from prospering, these are the levers to act on.' She looked around at the audience, taking care to make eye contact with each of them. *I like this, she remembers my instructions*, Wang Xiaobo thought.

'These were the major building blocks of HCBB.'

'I see that you've picked up a love of words yourself,' Luo Xiaosi interjected. He smiled kindly, so that it was clear he wasn't being sarcastic.

Chen Qingyang made that expression which Wang Xiaobo was familiar with, a sort of pressing of her lips which signalled a mental shrug. 'Well, Wang Xiaobo suggested I start with the principles,' she said.

'And I hope you don't follow all of his suggestions,' Luo Xiaosi said with a friendly grin.

Chen Qingyang tilted her head and raised her eyebrow. 'Well, I did turn down one, but that didn't seem to bother him much.'

For a second time, the room echoed with laughter. Wang Xiaobo kept a straight face. Chen Qingyang looked at him apologetically.

Luo Xiaosi thumped the table once. 'Okay, good for you. And him. Now let's go straight into the work breakdown structure.'

'Sure, Chief,' Chen Qingyang replied. She flicked a few holograms and came to one which had a neatly bulleted list, with headings numbered from 100 to 600.

'So here's the WBS. As you see, the first level breakdown had six major activity groups. I will take you through them without stopping. Kindly stop me if anything is not clear.' She looked at Ah Lan this time. *Yes, let him know you're ready for questions.*

'Activity 100 was defence industry harmonisation. HCBB had specific objectives here. Firstly, foreign weapons firms were subsidised so that they could pump bribes to Indian politicians. This was the biggest investment, but we believe that it was also the most successful one. There were dual benefits from the Indians not being able to make their large weapons, and a parallel black economy being developed.' The Brazil head and the man next to him bent toward each other, whispering. Luo Xiaosi looked at them and they straightened up like chastened schoolboys.

'Activity 200 was border harmonisation. Here we tried to improve the porosity factor of Indian borders. HCBB aimed at making larger cross-border movements possible with the cooperation of the relevant forces. Clear targets were set. It was planned that by 2029, it would be possible to take a tank across the border and back for ten thousand rupees. A steep learning curve was planned, under which a division of tanks would be taken across by 2034, where terrain permitted it, for twenty thousand rupees.'

Wang Xiaobo felt a rumble in his stomach. *Not surprising. I haven't eaten since I left the shuttle. It's better this way.* He was scared that his stomach would run if he ate.

'Activity 300 was governance harmonisation. Under this, as you can see, we had 310 for government, 320 for central and state parliaments, 330 for the judiciary and 340 for the police. The concept followed was the same in each. Entry barriers were first raised, then eased for the right kind of people to enter these jobs.' She pointed to the table. She had trimmed her nails and they were unpolished. 'The table here shows the target quotas. As you see, we preferred persons with more serious crime records for higher levels in each of the four arms. Yes?'

Ah Lan had a question. He shifted in his seat and cleared his throat. 'How were the quotas calculated?'

Chen Qingyang replied directly, 'I should know but I don't.' That was what Wang Xiaobo liked about her, the ability to say she didn't know. She turned toward him.

Wang Xiaobo stood up. 'Well, it's been a while now, so I'll have to look at the mathematical model, and I'm not sure even I can understand it.'

There were a few chuckles.

'But I can assure you that a friend at Tsinghua did the modelling. I remember that he used a technique called Data Envelopment Analysis to maximise the overall criminality in the system within our limited resources. We had weightages for different kinds of criminal backgrounds. In spite of our best efforts, there were some cases where uncooperative persons meandered into the systems. If there were too many of them, we ditched the math and just did them in.'

There was a polite round of laughter.

'And when we needed to take steps like that, we found tremendous benefits from the holistic nature of HCBB.' Wang Xiaobo signalled to Chen Qingyang as he sat down. 'Chen Qingyang.'

'Sure,' Chen Qingyang continued. 'Activity 400 was services and utilities. Under this we have 410, water; 420, electricity; 430, transport; 440, sanitation. 450, communication, was abandoned as it was difficult to stop mobile telephony. As for 410 to 440, these are self-explanatory and were not very resource-intensive once we had 300 under control. This group of activities actually turned out to be surplus-generating for us. For example, no electricity meant that generators were needed, and we were able to get a large indirect share of the generator market.'

Wang Xiaobo realised why he was feeling cold. He was clammy all over. *This will not do. Come on, get a grip on yourself!* He slowed his breath and felt a bit better.

'As far as roads were concerned, we made sure that they were made not to last. Also, a key feature of town planning in the shiny new towns was laid down by Wang Xiaobo. He stipulated that towns should be made such that people could not walk safely on the roads.' The graphic showed a street, without pavements, lined by glass buildings. A pedestrian had been hit by a car, and he lay there bleeding with the car speeding away.

'Activity 500 was one of the most important. It had 510, health, 520, education and 530, media. The objective here was the same as for 400. But because of the longer-term impact, these three were given special attention. Under health, the approach was to encourage the building of swanky new hospitals and pay doctors in government hospitals per hour of moonlighting. The rates were kept attractive. Fifty thousand nursing homes were set up and given targets for unnecessary operations and organ collection. The organs they collected on the side and shipped to China helped us to increase our life expectancy to its current level of 120 years. This remains a lasting benefit of HCBB. Also, they had a clear target to reduce the percentage of natural childbirths to zero, which they met easily.'

Wang Xiaobo felt much better already. *I'm glad I was born when I was. And thank God for HCBB, whatever they conclude today.*

'520, education, was similarly directed at making education irrelevant and useless. Two major thrusts were taken here. First, a programme was started to have one thousand IITs, after we found that we could not easily degrade the existing ones. Second, a large-scale programme was launched to have one million MBA colleges in the country. Some academics were guided to propose that instead of math, class 5 students should be taught Porter's five forces analysis and other such subjects from management.' The graphic showed two double-storied buildings, separated by a big MacDonald's outlet, in a crowded market area. One was called International Business Institute, and the other Nehru Management Institute. Both advertised that they offered BBA, CBA, MBA and DBA degrees.

'Of course, 530, media, was what made a lot of this possible. Wang Xiaobo modestly says that he cannot take credit for most Indian journalists of that time being idiots.'

A few people in the room guffawed. Chen Qingyang looked surprised. 'No, it's true, he doesn't. However, HCBB did help to make sure that the media was loud, unthinking and completely corrupt. Some snapshots of the Indian media in action are in Appendix 3. Journalists were encouraged to use the word "superpower" in every fourth article, and to make comparisons with us based on seminal papers by

India-China experts who rarely stepped out of their college campuses in the US.' She cleared her throat and took a sip of water. Wang Xiaobo looked at the glass in front of him. He was thirsty, but he couldn't bring himself to drink. There was a knot in his stomach, and he had a feeling that it would only go when he pressed the trigger and got the hell out of this place.

'Finally, we come to 600, sports and culture. Under 610, sports, it was enough to keep the Indian crazy after cricket. This game helped to increase paunchiness and reduce overall alertness. Our friends in the media helped us no end. We got the Indian Olympic Association to ask for a game called Antakshari to be made an Olympic sport. Under 620, overall behaviour, we organised a pay per activity scheme. In strategic locations, we paid people to shit in the open, spit and piss freely, grope anyone they could and beg even if they weren't starving.' The graphic now showed a row of men peeing against a wall, with a congested street behind them. 'When HCBB operatives started to explain this, they faced a lot of scepticism—people didn't believe they could get paid for stuff they were doing anyway. One of our operatives even got beaten up for making an offer. But it paid off in the long run, and 620 actually became our preferred means of inserting fake currency notes into the economy.'

Ah Lan half raised his hand, but then dropped it. 'The activity 630, film, was started but abandoned as Bollywood films were crappy enough without our intervention, and on the other hand, their music was quite superb in spite of our best efforts. However, we did continue with 640, film appreciation. Under this we encouraged Bollywood dancing to become the cultural staple of India. I'd like to take you to Appendix 4 to show you a sample...'

She thumbed a few buttons, and a video came up. It showed little boys making pelvic thrusts and skimpily dressed little girls wriggling their still flat chests to Bollywood songs under the approving gazes of a crowd of elderly people, presumably their parents. Wang Xiaobo and Chen Qingyang were unaffected, but the rest of the group, even Luo Xiaosi, gaped at it.

'So that's what it's like. The last subactivity under 600 was 640, debating. Under this, we sponsored one debate a year in each of the top thousand towns of India. Wang Xiaobo recognised that to the Indian mind, a person who had spent his life farting around in a UN job was a great intellectual. 640 was aimed at spreading this love of debating. For the motion, against the motion. Wonderful commotion.' She smiled, for the first time, and her pride in their work shone through.

There were loud chuckles and a few whispers.

'Well, there you have it,' Chen Qingyang said after it was quiet. 'And this visual shows you the top level WBS with all activities. Questions?'

The room was silent.

Luo Xiaosi sighed. 'No need for questions, Chen Qingyang. Let's move on to the status update of 2029, and then get to today.'

IV

'SURE, CHIEF,' Chen Qingyang continued. 'By 2029, and I was around by then, HCBB had become a great success. On some dimensions, the achievements were incredible.'

She displayed a map of South Asia and said, 'Border porosity had been achieved completely. On 15 August 2029, a tank division crossed over the Bangladesh-India border at Hilli, here, and travelled mostly in a train to the Pakistan-India border point, here, in sixty-three days. This was a proud moment for us, a new long march. It meant that we had made Mughalstan happen at a reasonable cost.'

Then she flicked the remote and the hologram changed to a pair of pictures, one showing a team of smiling, formally dressed men signing a document at a large table, and the other of a bunch of unkempt, thuggish looking men with their arms and legs sprawled out so that they filled the frame of the picture.

'The Greater Asian Lead Acceleration Treaty had been signed, under which India agreed to make Southern Tibet, which they called by the funny name of Arunachal Pradesh, an autonomous region operated by China in return for a seat on the UN Security Council.' She motioned toward a link beneath the picture. 'This link points to a video clip that shows the celebration in the streets of Delhi after this Security Council appointment. That thing the people are doing is a dance called the Bhangra.'

Wang Xiaobo had suggested that she avoid showing the video in the interest of time management. He would have liked to flash it, though, just for entertainment value. 'On the same day, Naxalite rebels in the states of Chattisgarh and Jharkhand hijacked four trains and released all prisoners from ten prisons after announcing a general amnesty. That didn't figure in the news.' The graphic showed dozens of men in dark fatigues, brandishing some heavy-looking weaponry including rocket launchers, charging toward a white building with a flat facade. The front of the building had a gaping hole from which smoke billowed out.

'While we were taking these defensive actions in cooperation with the Pakistanis, we also sponsored several peace initiatives. Most of these were led by the noted intellectual socialite, Rosanna Dey-Bhatt, shown here fully dressed.'

The hologram changed to show an attractive, auburn-haired, fair woman dressed in a shimmering sari. She was surrounded by glitterati.

There were a few titters in the room.

Wang Xiaobo interrupted: 'It's interesting that this lady, Dey-Bhatt, spent considerable time with her butt connected to my Pakistani counterpart.'

Ah Lan quipped, 'Hey Wang Xiaobo, how the hell do you know? Did she tell you?'

'Well, to be honest,' Wang Xiaobo replied, 'she had me in her mouth as well, most of those times.'

They exploded with laughter, but Wang Xiaobo noticed Chen Qingyang's stony look. She was looking at Luo Xiaosi, whose face was unusually white.

It didn't take long for everyone to quiet down. There was a moment's silence.

'Wang Xiaobo, we are aware of your activities on the—the procreational front.' Luo Xiaosi's words carried an inflection which signalled anger. 'I'm not sure that's the right word but I don't want to be crude.'

Luo Xiaosi was known to be a bit of a prude, and a one-woman man. 'I have to ask you this: please don't divert the discussion!' He ended the sentence loudly and his words had the effect of a whip.

Wang Xiaobo noticed the satisfied look on Ah Lan's face and the sympathy on Chen Qingyang's.

Luo Xiaosi continued: 'I think I know what you're thinking. You're probably thinking about the fact that Li Yinhe left you for me, and that I have no right to lecture you on decadence...'

The room went quieter. The rest of the team was stunned. They hadn't expected this.

Wang Xiaobo's mind had gone blank for a moment. He collected and focused his thoughts. *You really don't know what I'm thinking. I'll be happier to kill you now. There are other things you don't know. It's strange but when I think about it now, I'm not ashamed that I miss her. I miss the peace of resting my head in the valley of her arm, shoulder and breast. And funnily enough, the smell of her. Even after all the women I've had but that I couldn't sleep with. So, Luo Xiaosi, when this meeting ends, I will ask to stay back.* On its own, his right hand reached for the gun, stroking it and drawing solace from it. *And I will kill you. I might shoot your knees first, instead of doing it cleanly*. He took a deep breath, stretched and interlocked his fingers behind his back.

Luo Xiaosi's voice was measured again. 'Chen Qingyang, please bring us up to speed on LKY and the current situation. You can continue with the historical element, though, as that is important.' He looked around the room. 'No interruptions, please.' He zeroed in on Wang Xiaobo. 'Wang Xiaobo, will you stay back after the meeting? There's something I need to talk over.'

Wang Xiaobo looked calmly into Luo Xiaosi's eyes and bowed slightly. 'Sure, Chief. Actually, I was making a conceptual point about the parallels between what the two of us did to Dey-Bhatt and what we were doing to that country. You got me wrong.'

Luo Xiaosi slumped. 'After the meeting, please.'

Wang Xiaobo nodded. *You bet*.

Chen Qingyang continued: 'India was buying weapons worth a hundred-odd billion yuan every year. After accounting for transmission losses, seventy percent of that amount flowed to us. This chart shows the cumulative sales generated.' She pointed at the chart and took a minute to explain the axes labels and some of the finer points. Wang Xiaobo lost interest for a while. For some reason, he remembered Li Yinhe as he had last seen her. She had always looked beautiful when she was angry. *Come on, get a grip*.

'There were thirty-nine states,' Chen Qingyang was saying when he focused again, 'in line with our blueprint. These graphics show the progressive breaking up of the states from 1947 to 2029. Note that there was some blowback from the formation of smaller states—it made the centre relatively stronger and the smaller states were slightly better governed than their larger parent states had been. In Wang Xiaobo's view, this was one of our first failures.'

Wang Xiaobo had let his mind drift again to the time when Li Yinhe had walked out of his flat, taking nothing with her. She would burn the clothes she was wearing later, she had said. He willed himself back into the presentation.

'However, there were huge successes. There were serious terrorist strikes once every three years. After every strike, the newspapers spewed venom at the politicians, soldiers had their leaves cancelled, and entire corps were marched to the borders.' She flicked to a new hologram, which showed tanks churning up the sand as they charged through a desert.

'These graphics show the movements of 2029, just for example. A warlike situation was declared with Pakistan and a red alert was called. Then the peace brigade called for a cricket match, and the tension started to dissolve. The main outcome of these warlike activities was substantial spending on fuel, which again indirectly flowed to us.' She beamed and looked at Luo Xiaosi, who nodded encouragement.

'Most heads of the police and the judiciary were selected for having serious criminal backgrounds.' She flicked the remote and the hologram changed to show a uniformed man walking out of a crowded doorway.

'Here you can see a head of police smiling as he walks out of a Major Court. He's been acquitted by a judge whose conscience wouldn't allow him to convict a fellow rapist.'

'Meanwhile, we had argued for more Indians to be given Nobel prizes. One of the Brown Sahibs who won the Nobel Prize for literature said in his acceptance speech that literature written in Indian languages was insignificant. This was an encouraging statement for us. You can see it in this graphic.' She flicked to a new graphic showing a very intelligent-looking, hirsute man and a quote in golden letters. 'Its importance should not be underestimated.'

Ah Lan raised his hand. 'Didn't he become unpopular for that? We would have...' He shrugged.

'No,' she said, 'he seems to have done fine. And there's more.' She flicked to a new graphic, showing another man, who was bald with pointy hair above his ears. 'Another great intellectual, an economist and management thinker, showed that there was a statistically significant relationship between a vibrant domestic porn industry and economic prosperity. He used structural equation modelling and showed that his model was supported by all the relevant Goodness--of-Fit statistics. This diagram'—she paused to show a very rigorous looking graphic full of arrows, boxes and numbers—'is from his paper in the *Forward Business Review*.' Wang Xiaobo realised that the print was a bit too small. On the other hand, it made everyone lean forward to make an effort to read, which was good.

'Much of this was the planned outcome of the WBS activities 100 to 600, which I have explained earlier. Overall, HCBB had been incredibly successful by 2029.

Without going into the complex linkages between the project activities and the resulting benefits, here is a summary of these achievements, backed by the relevant data. Please stop me if something is not clear.' She changed the graphic to a bulleted slide which showed a long list of achievements.

'Firstly, defence of the realm had been compromised. Secondly, law enforcement was satisfactorily hopeless. I have provided some examples from these two areas earlier. In addition, public utilities were nonexistent. Only the top one percent of the population had access to good healthcare. The country was mostly powered by biodiesel generators for which we supplied most of the components and fuel. We had encouraged the use of larger flushes by the rich—you can see a sample here, which consumes twenty litres of water per flush—and we optimised cistern size so that it was twice the average per capita availability of water.' The graphic showed pictures of cistern sizes every five years, and it was clear that the sizes had increased satisfactorily.

'On the political front, there were two main parties, the Regress Party and the Janta Bajao Party. The first was a bit better at graft, and the second at pogroms, but they were both quite suitable from our point of view. In addition, there were about 137 smaller parties. Together, these parties had plundered more money than Mahmud of Ghazni, Muhammad Ghori, Nadir Shah, Ahmad Shah Abdali and the

British put together, even after adjusting for the time value of money.'

A number of hands went up, and Chen Qingyang used the break to gulp down the rest of the water in her glass. Luo Xiaosi had slumped a bit, and he straightened up now. 'I guess you'll want to know what that means,' he said.

Ah Lan, one of those who had raised his hand, nodded and was about to say something. Luo Xiaosi stopped him by making a braking action with his hand, pumping it in the air with his palm outward. 'Let's skip the history lesson, okay?' He smiled. 'I think what Chen Quingyang wants to say is that those parties had established a good track record. Right?' He looked at Chen Qingyang, who bowed to express consent. He nodded for her to carry on.

She flicked the remote to get to a new graphic, which showed a rotund man in white, surrounded by about twenty fierce-looking bodyguards in black. 'Here you can see how the politicians travelled, surrounded by gun-toting commandoes. While the editors we paid wrote powerful editorials on India being the world's largest democracy, the gap between the government and the people widened every day.'

'The monthly sum of farmer suicides and female foetus murders, which we arranged to be called gender selection, was a Fibonacci series. You can see the three curves here—farmer suicide events, gender selection events and the total events.' The hologram this time was a simple-time series, with a red line, a blue one and a thicker black one. She paused so that they could take it in.

'Our efforts in education produced results. The MBA institutes produced shitloads of MBAs who had no takers. Most of them started to work for escort services, which had become the largest employer in the country. Many graduates from the thousand IITs became call centre employees. The percentage of the population which had access to primary schooling actually dropped from forty in 2009, when we started work, to twenty-nine in 2029. In 2009, 2019 and 2029 our people in the parliament helped to draft lengthier bills assuring universal education.' The graphic showed three monstrously large books, with their covers engraved with the words 'The Right of Children to Free and Compulsory Education Act.'

'Gradually, a loose body of intellectuals from government, industry, academia, media and the arts started to get a stranglehold on the nation. As we anticipated, only about half of them were intelligent enough so that we needed to incentivise them. Most of them were plain stupid and worked for us for free.'

Wang Xiaobo raised his hand. Chen Qingyang nodded for him to speak. 'I wanted to emphasise,' he said, 'that catalysing the formation of this body was a great achievement. It was informally called the Knowledge Workers and Media Savants Association, KAMSA. It never had a formal presence, but it had a lot of soft power. If there was one achievement which I used to take personal pride in, it was in the formation of this KAMSA.'

Wang Xiaobo nodded, and Chen Qingyang continued. The graphic had changed to a neat bulleted list. 'Here you can see some key points from an important event: the so-called Delhi gang rape of 16 December 2029. In summary, what happened was that a 23-year-old woman was gang raped by six men in a bus in Delhi. In fact, rape had become common by then, but this case became a bit hot. Only for a few months, of course.' Chen Qingyang gulped.

Wang Xiaobo had been worried about this bit—she had come close to quitting when it happened.

'The thing is that the rape was brutal enough, given that a rod was also used in the process, but what followed was the culmination of our efforts of many decades. The Chief Minister of Delhi, a woman, said that the woman had been too adventurous. The media fanned the usual hot air, and a journalist working for the Network News Cable wrote an article titled "Indian Men Should be Taught Not to Rape." The poor woman was packed off to Singapore, which was pretty much a death sentence. They could have sent her to the national hospital AIIMS, across the road, which we had not been able to infiltrate. And the debates went on: for the motion, against the motion. There were protests in the streets during which two more rapes occurred.' Her voice was a bit hoarse. Wang Xiaobo was concerned.

'In the end, the youngest of the rapists got away with a three-year prison term. No one talked about the one thing that could have saved the woman: effective beat patrolling. Actually, the police had information that those rapists were drunk and loose on the streets in a bus, two hours before they picked that woman up.'

Wang Xiaobo had expected Ah Lan to butt in. He did. 'How comfortable were you with the ethics of all this?' he asked.

Chen Qingyang's face fell. Wang Xiaobo noticed that her fingers trembled a bit. *This will not do*, he thought. *How will you survive after I've lit out?* 'I'll take that,' he said aloud. 'To answer your question, Chen Qingyang sent me a resignation message. I'll summarise my advice to her: we did not rape anyone. What happened to the woman was ... bad, but they did it. We had our ethics policy, of course, and we stayed within it. In particular, one of the policy clauses, 420, made it clear what we should do on a tricky ethics issue. We should ask: if God was an ISI chief, what would he want the Indian leaders to do?'

Ah Lan recoiled. 'How the hell did you figure that?'

'We asked, of course,' Wang Xiaobo replied.

'You asked God?' Ah Lan kept his voice low and his face straight, but he couldn't suppress a chuckle.

'No, the ISI chief,' Wang Xiaobo said. He hoped his smirk didn't show. 'He was on our payroll, remember?'

Ah Lan looked crushed.

Wang Xiaobo thought he might as well rub it in. 'You had eyes, but you didn't recognise Mount Taishan, huh?'

Ah Lan looked away, and Wang Xiaobo stood up and stretched. He enjoyed feeling the rub of the gun in the small of his back. His spine was troubling him. It wasn't screaming yet, but he had needed that stretch. He was fit for an 80-year-old, but, what the hell, he wasn't young any more. He continued: 'This story is probably getting a bit boring. I think Chen Qingyang has summarised our work well. She has more material, but I propose we move on to the part where HCBB started to fail.'

There were murmurs of agreement. Luo Xiaosi nodded.

'Sure,' said Chen Qingyang.

'I would like to remind you of the phenomenon that we were not able to counter—feedback.' Wang Xiaobo said. 'We did excellent work in altering the design of a system, but the system responded in ways which we could not have countered—because we could not imagine the responses. I know there will be some of you here who will have a lot of wisdom to offer on this.'

They were all quiet. Wang Xiaobo imagined the deafening commotion that would have filled the room if their thought phones were on.

Luo Xiaosi cleared his throat. 'I think it's clear that you did good work.' He spoke with his hands clasped. 'We also have to remember that the scope of the project was quite large. We tried to harmonise the behaviour of their one billion people with the interests of our one billion. I signed on the project blueprints, and as you say, Wang Xiaobo, we didn't account for feedback because we didn't know what we didn't know.'

Wang Xiaobo noticed how Chen Qingyang's facial muscles relaxed. The gap between her eyebrows widened infinitesimally. He had mastered these signals over the years. *Is that how she reacts when she's kissed on the forehead?*

'Anyhow,' Luo Xiaosi continued, 'I guess the subject Chen Qingyang will now take is Lal Kant Yadav. Or LKY, as he came to be called. Correct?'

'Yes, Chief,' Chen Qingyang replied as she flicked past a few graphics. Wang Xiaobo sat down.

V

THE NEXT GRAPHIC showed a dark man. There was something weird about his darkness—it had a tinge of blue. He stood with his hands folded in a namaste amidst rows of benches full of people dressed in white. Then a video started. The dark man spoke and was heard in pin-drop silence by the people in the video. In the meeting room as well, there was rapt attention.

The video was paused. 'I thought this was a good place to start the section,' Chen Qingyang said. 'This is LKY's first speech in the Indian parliament, the Lok Sabha. The people you see there are the Members of Parliament, and most of them were working for us. Or so we thought.' She took a deep breath.

Yes, it's strange how much events diverged from our plans, Wang Xiaobo thought.

'But we were wrong. More on that later. This is the speech which changed everything. You will see the details in the subtitles, but let me explain what happened that day. LKY made four announcements.' She reached for her empty glass of water again. Wang Xiaobo stood up and carried his glass over. He wouldn't be drinking it anyway. She smiled and bowed. He turned back toward his chair, and she started off.

'First, he announced that the Indian government had traced enough stolen funds in foreign and domestic accounts to cover eight years of GDP. These funds were being demanded by the Indian treasury in equal monthly instalments.' She looked at Luo Xiaosi, who maintained his stony expression.

'I'm letting excerpts from his speech play on now.' The team watched, fascinated as LKY spoke in a language which was unfamiliar to all of them except for Wang Xiaobo and Chen Qingyang.

'Second,' Chen Qingyang continued, 'he linked the salary of the President to corporate packages. It was double the average of the top ten corporate packages, actually. All pay scales were revised in line with the President's. MPs got reelection bonuses which were shared with their parties. Notice the looks on the MPs' faces.'

The MPs looked dazed. One of them seemed to be punching figures on his tablet, scratching his head once in a while.

'Third, LKY announced that taxes would be simplified. Income tax was replaced with an expenditure tax on a specific list of fifty products and services. In addition, there were only four kinds of taxes—customs duty, goods and service tax, share and commodity transaction tax and property transfer and ownership tax.' Wang Xiaobo made the sign to move on faster, rolling his finger. 'I'll skip the details here.

Fourth, all military R&D projects were given timelines to deliver their products. LKY made a simple statement: that the government would not pay twice for the same thing. If a product had to be imported, R&D would be stopped. On the other hand, the cost savings from indigenous development would be shared with the people who delivered the savings.'

'Are there questions?' Chen Qingyang asked. They were all silent. Ah Lan fidgeted, and looked like he might say something.

Wang Xiaobo butted in. 'I think the logic of these steps is pretty clear, but the question is, how did LKY come onto the scene?'

Ah Lan raised his hand, and Chen Qingyang nodded. 'My friend,' he said, 'the real question is how come we couldn't just knock him off?'

Wang Xiaobo sighed and stood up. 'I'll answer that, as I think I am responsible. The thing is that it's not as if we didn't try. But the dice were loaded one way.' *Where do I start?* He folded his hands and thought for a while.

'Let me start with LKY's birth and upbringing. He was born to a rich industrialist couple in a god-forsaken town in the part of the country called the cowbelt. We don't even know how the hell he made it out alive. His mother had had seven miscarriages before him. He did not leave the hospital with his birth mother. By this time, we had implemented hospital management systems which enabled mixing of babies. It was one of our subactivities under the WBS code 510. He ended up getting shunted to a slum called Lukog, in exchange for a sickly baby from there who died within a day.' He felt Luo Xiaosi's gaze on him, and held it for a while before engaging the others in the audience.

'The thing is, by the time he appeared on our radar, he had a charmed life and a band of faithful followers. He was sixteen then, and he held sway over a largish party of principled Outlaws of the Marsh who extorted money, but were very popular with the poor. They stayed away from prostitution and drugs, and in fact one of the things which made them popular was that they broke the arms and legs of operatives who were into human trafficking.' Wang Xiaobo's hand wandered to the small of his back. He was tempted to feel the gun one more time, but he resisted the temptation.

'At this stage, I have to confess I still did not track him personally. But someone in Chen Qingyang's team did an issue erase order. It's just our luck, but the first two guys sent to erase him, one on a scooter and the other in a car, both died in accidents. To an extent, this was the outcome of our efforts in traffic management.' Out of the corner of his eye, he saw Ah Lan raise his hand, but he looked away.

'Then we sent a girl. He's known to be irresistible to women, something about his looks. Also, it's stated that he has an incredible ability to make them squirt.'

Luo Xiaosi cleared his throat.

Wang Xiaobo shrugged. 'So, we sent this girl with poisoned nipple tips to him. As it turned out, he had been given adulterated medicines all his life, under WBS 510. The poison should have screwed up his biological systems, and maybe it did screw up his mind. But he survived it. In the exchange of body fluids that took place when they mated, strangely, the girl died. LKY's complexion changed into the blue-black one which he has now. That should have made him unattractive, but oddly, it didn't.' He looked at Chen Qingyang, who was taking notes. Sometimes he thought she really overdid the earnestness.

'When he was only 21,' he continued, 'and on the verge of winning an election, Chen Qingyang briefed me about him, and I confess that in the larger scheme of things he still appeared insignificant. Still, I authorised a Snake missile strike on his slum hut. Does anyone need a brief on the Snake missile?'

'We'll skip that,' Luo Xiaosi said.

'Okay.' Wang Xiaobo shrugged. 'Well, our run of luck continued. The Snake missile hit the hut, but it had rained all day and the slum was a slush pile. The drain running through it had turned into a river, and the load didn't explode. I'm told LKY sat on the missile shell as it floated in the river and calmly gave his troops a talk. And then he drank himself silly and danced in a trance. On that Snake missile.'

'Just tell us how many attempts you made,' Luo Xiaosi said.

'We made a total of seven. It happened suddenly that he grew too big even for us to knock out. He had all these troops, and there was this other guy RBY, Ram Bal Yadav, who became his guide and friend. We couldn't buy or bump off any of the people close to him. His location became a well-kept secret. It's incredible, but within ten years, he was making this speech as Prime Minister.' He pointed to the still of LKY making the speech in parliament.

'Tell us what happened to all your other achievements, like the KAMSA,' Luo Xiaosi said. He was leaning forward, with his chin resting on his joined hands.

'Well,' Wang Xiaobo said, 'first of all, the KAMSA was the product of irreconcilable class antagonisms, and it withered away as LKY and his team grew more active. Apart from that, in his stint as minister, LKY got some things done. For example, he got giant force shields installed at traffic lights, and cars that jumped them got smashed. He also set up decoy operations, mostly rape bait ops, in which his chosen honest cops whacked the hell out of the hoodlums who had the country by its balls. Many people affected in those ops were policemen and politicians—we lost several good people—but some were members of KAMSA.' He started to pace around his chair to relieve his knees.

'He reduced the maximum denomination of rupee notes from one million rupees to a thousand, and it became a nightmare to manage cash logistics. A lot of our operatives ended up with slipped discs.'

It was interesting that at least two people in the audience massaged their backs at the mention of slipped discs.

'He also made it compulsory to have a two-minute silence on TV and radio every time there was a terrorist attack or other tragedy of any kind. The TV anchors and RJs went into depression after a few such silences, and that weakened KAMSA, as well. The ones who went in for medical treatment came back with schizophrenia, due to our success in the health systems area.'

'How the hell did this silence thing reduce terrorist attacks?' Ah Lan asked.

'It didn't,' Wang Xiaobo replied. 'A few other things did. LKY got bounty hunters to assassinate our agents in Pakistan who gave the jihadis their orders. That was all it took to stop them—those guys had been merrily pulling triggers without feeling the recoil. LKY turned the fire on them with five assassinations, and then signed agreements with twelve separatist organisations within India. The Naxalite terror died away in about five years, while LKY started ethical mining and stopped the plunder of the forest areas.'

'And you let the jihadis starve?' Ah Lan looked around. It was obvious he was trying to score points.

Wang Xiaobo saw Chen Qingyang start to turn a bit red. He spoke with measured words. 'No, we stayed true to them. We got them recruited into politics in Pakistan.'

'And the intellectual who did the porn study, you know, the guy you showed?' Luo Xiaosi asked.

'Yes, unfortunately, LKY personally showed him a movie with his own children in it. The guy became a vegetable.'

'And did we abandon him?' Luo Xiaosi asked.

'Oh, no,' Wang Xiaobo was emphatic. 'We got that guy into the National Intelligence Agency. LKY shifted him to the Planning Commission, where he didn't make a difference to output. Later, we found some of our main partners getting shunted out of posts where they could be of use to us.'

'I remember this bit about a guardian angel from one of your dispatches. Tell them about that,' Luo Xiaosi said.

Wang Xiaobo sighed. 'Yes, I didn't like sending it. But it was verified information. We figured that there must be a source which inspired him. A source we could hit out at. It turned out that he acknowledged an angel, a woman wearing a white dress with some markings in saffron and green, who appeared to him in his dreams. It sounds crazy, but that is how it has been this last decade.'

'And what followed is history?' Luo Xiaosi asked. 'Yes. Chen Qingyang has graphics and videos.

There's been a surge of development after that bloody speech. LKY took a gamble and it worked. But apart from those four steps, there's also more that they've done, like in the railways—they're on track to increasing their railway route kilometres from one fourth of ours to just below ours. They'll have 170,000 route kilometres soon. A grid of rail freight lines with RORO facilities connects Delhi, Mumbai, Bengaluru,

Kolkata and Dispur. A truck can cover Delhi--Bengaluru or Delhi-Dispur in twelve hours.' *Who could have imagined it, even twenty short years ago?* He thought.

He continued, 'Their decentralised electricity programme has powered up ninety-five percent of their villages. The biggest rivers have been cleaned up, and those fuckers have managed to implement watershed management systems with better returns and less damage than our bloody dams. Last year Mumbai was ranked the third most liveable city in the world, after Vienna and Vancouver.' He looked at Chen Qingyang, and she pulled out a graphic which showed the ranking of cities.

'There's been a flurry of branded non-shitty products,' said Wang Xiaobo, 'like this watch I'm wearing, these bloody hand-cranked lamps you see in the graphic. Within a decade, LKY set up more than a hundred Indian Institutes of Health, IIHs, about one per ten million people. There's one large Central Technician Institute in every district and one Central Primary School giving meals to children in every village block and city ward. Do you have something on them?' he asked Chen Qingyang.

She nodded and pulled up a graphic which showed an aerial view of a huge green campus. The caption said that it was the hundredth IIH.

'They have won contracts for their stealth fighter, the Vyom, from the UK, Russia and France. They've even won seventeen gold medals in the Moscow Olympics.'

The display showed a sleek-looking fighter jet blazing a white trail across a clear blue sky.

'LKY got the states to do what he had experimented with earlier: recruit millions of employees to the police, judiciary and essential services without any bribery. We had designed some pretty robust systems, but we found they couldn't handle this sudden shock.' He felt a bit tired now. He could go on, but he wanted to have energy left over after the meeting was done. His stomach rumbled again. *Be honest. It's fear. But it's all right.*

'Chen Qingyang, did you have something to add?' asked Wang Xiaobo.

'Lots of material to show, Chief, but nothing much to add really,' Chen Qingyang said. 'I can say that Delhi has become dangerously safe for women. Even for women from the Indian North East, who used to be called Chinkies in the good old days of the 2020s. Some friends of mine, stewardesses on Singapore Airlines, told me they vie to get on flights to India. Of course, these are minor things…' she trailed off when Luo Xiaosi had signalled her to stop. The room was quiet. Luo Xiaosi was stoic.

'So, where do we go from here, Chief?' Ah Lan asked. He kept his voice level. There was no taunt.

Wang Xiaobo sat down. His tiredness was a bad sign. The next hour was crucial. He hoped they wouldn't be hard on Chen Qingyang. The commas check would show her clear, but you never knew. *What will it feel like? To pull the trigger on someone whom I loved and hated? And who saved my life?*

Luo Xiaosi was looking at him. 'Well?'

'I'm sorry, Chief, I wasn't listening,' Wang Xiaobo was apologetic.

'Where do we go from here?' Luo Xiaosi asked with a detached look.

'There's nowhere to go, Chief. The rumour is LKY knows about us. And I've sensed that... It's difficult to be sure, but I've sensed that we're being watched.'

'Is that how we work now? Sense things?' Ah Lan asked. He was smirking.

The words continued. They would not debate for long, Wang Xiaobo knew. He took part in it, but a part of him was about to switch off.

Luo Xiaosi stood up. The room went quiet. Wang Xiaobo heard the sound of his own breath and the noise in his head. *It's surprising. He's a larger-than-life figure for us. And he's all of 165 centimetres. Look at the lines on his forehead. And that funny lump that's forming below his eye.*

'We will treat this as a project closeout meeting,' Luo Xiaosi said. 'Chen Qingyang, please submit the project closeout report within the usual time of four weeks for a megaproject.' Chen Qingyang bowed. 'You will probably want me to comment on our work,' he said. 'Where did we go wrong? I went wrong in the beginning, in 2009. We didn't need an HCBB. I fell for the "India Shining" crap. I should have known better. The Indians already had a KAMSA of sorts. They stewed in the filth their leaders kept them in, and loved it.' He had a spaced-out look now, as if he was looking over their heads into the far distance.

'Much before we started HCBB,' he went on, 'there was a terrorist attack on their parliament. I was shocked when I talked to a guy I knew and he said it was a pity the terrorists were so dumb they didn't get any of the MPs. First, I thought this guy was anomalous, but when I probed deeper I found every Indian felt that way. Everyone, no exceptions.' He jabbed the air with his index finger. 'I knew this.'

'Around the time we extracted the Letter of the Two Sorries from the Americans over a spy plane incident, the Indians decided to take it easy and not get too sentimental when the Bangladeshis tortured sixteen of their soldiers to death.' He jabbed the air again. 'I knew this.'

'I knew that while their Railway Minister Khaaloon Prasad was touring the leading universities of the world and staying in the leading hotels of the world, collecting Best CEO awards for turning around their railways, the shit was piling up on the tracks and they called a train superfast if it did 55 kilometres an hour. I knew that this was a country in which a bestselling book sold five thousand copies. I knew that their intellectuals would get misty-eyed at the mention of Iwo Jima or Dien Bien Phu, but knew fuck all about Chushul or Mount Popa.' Luo Xiaosi made that gesture with his finger again, shook his head and exhaled. 'And I knew these intellectuals were proud of reading Ayn Rand.'

Wang Xiaobo looked around the room. Each one of them sat ramrod straight, or leaned forward. This was one of Luo Xiaosi's longest-ever speeches. He usually wasn't so theatrical.

'Even worse,' he continued, 'HCBB got us the wrong outcome. We started a project to destabilise and we made it work so well that it stabilised. This is nature. There is feedback, and it is not always possible to know it before it has happened. It is easy to say that once the instability crossed a threshold, if it wasn't LKY, someone else would have come in. The point is we haven't seen anyone else like that. So, let's set the theorising aside and be thankful that we made money.' He smiled, and, almost as if on cue, Ah Lan and two others laughed.

'Are there questions?' He looked at Ah Lan. No one spoke.

Luo Xiaosi sat down, and that was the end of the meeting. Wang Xiaobo felt Chen Qingyang's gaze on him. He gave Chen Qingyang his usual salute. He sensed her disappointment that he had not walked up and complimented her. Time seemed to spurt when he wanted it to slow down. Too soon, they were all shuffling out.

Then there were the two of them: Luo Xiaosi and Wang Xiaobo.

Luo Xiaosi was at the head of the table, and Wang Xiaobo was on his left, three chairs away. Wang Xiaobo had thought he would sweat or tremble. He did not. He held the QSZ40 in his hand and felt its cold butt against his thumb. Luo Xiaosi could not see it under the table.

Luo Xiaosi sat slumped for a longish time after the door had closed. He seemed to be making his mind up about something. Then he signalled to Wang Xiaobo to turn his thought phone on.

VI

AFTER THE OLD man from Delhi office went in, Luo Zi was lost in thought for a while. What was it about him? She was used to attracting men, that was no problem. She wasn't exactly repulsed by him. The thought irritated her. She should have been.

She could leave now, as she had completed her quota of two hours. Her thoughts wandered to Zhong He, and to the room upstairs, and she felt a kind of hunger. She called him with her thought phone.

What's up? He seemed puzzled. She had told him she would be doing hourly work. She never said more than that.

Don't know. Can you get down here?

Why?

What do you think?

I have to submit a progress report tomorrow. He was studying for a Ph.D. at Tsinghua and the fate of his scholarship had always been a bit tenuous, unlike hers. She didn't mind helping him out, but his pride came in the way.

Will you get down here, please? At the office?

He sighed. *It'll take me an hour at least. I have to fuel the scooter.*

I'm waiting. Get to the room upstairs.

She watched a movie on her cube, an old Hong Kong flick, *2046*, remastered from 2D but still grainy. It was convoluted but engrossing. And some parts were incredibly erotic.

She made her way up to the room when it was time. The wait was irritating. She felt the itch building up and she fought it.

It was slightly more than an hour when Zhong He's black scooter passed the window and then turned back. He docked it in the port outside and climbed in. The building was old and not air--transport-friendly.

He had his back toward her when he manoeuvred himself in. He wore a new white T-shirt, and its label stuck out from the neck. She admired his leanness as he turned around.

They looked at each other. His hair was dishevelled from the wind and the pressure of the helmet. She broke into a smile.

Get naked.

He folded his hands across his chest and stared at her.

And switch off your thought phone.

He stood there with his hands folded, thinking. She could feel the anger building up in him. This would be good.

In a second, he had jumped forward and wrestled her to the floor. He was only a bit stronger. She tapped the floor twice, but he disregarded the signal.

Switch off our thought phones, idiot.

He held her wrists with one hand and switched them off. She could have got her hands free, but she didn't. He was still struggling for words. She laughed.

He cleared his throat. 'Okay,' he said. 'Repeat after me: a woman's place is below her man.'

She pouted in the way she knew he liked, and said, 'Your mother's place is below your neighbour.' She laughed as he took the words in, slowly, and his gaze hardened. She hoped he would last.

VII

THEIR THOUGHTS WERE silent. Time had slowed down. When Wang Xiaobo looked up after switching his thought phone on, Luo Xiaosi was standing. It took Wang Xiaobo a couple of seconds to register that there was something wrong.

I see you have a gun pointing at me! Wang Xiaobo couldn't hide his surprise. He gripped his own gun tighter.

True. Laser QSZ30. Luo Xiaosi was phlegmatic. *Old but reliable, like me. It'll do the job. The rules allow me to come in armed.*

It wouldn't have been easy for you to shoot me anyway, Chief, but don't be in a hurry. You see—

I'm not in a hurry, Wang Xiaobo, I'm not. I'll tell you why first. You already know.

Chief, I brought in a QSZ40. I have it right here pointing at your guts. May I bring it up to show you?

She let me down. Luo Xiaosi's forehead was furrowed.

The girl?

Yes.

She's pretty. I guess you don't...

She's my daughter.

I didn't know. Wang Xiaobo's instincts told him to stop there. It was difficult.

I see you got your finger to the trigger.

True, Chief. How do you think we'll get out of this?

It's too early to say. Luo Zi?

Is that her name?

Luo Zi? She let me down again. Luo Xiaosi smiled wanly. *Yes, that's her name. By the way, I know about you. You're probably wondering about me. I got an alert on the transfer to your Singapore account.*

So, you were tracking my accounts. I'm disappointed. Wang Xiaobo beamed.

I track everyone's.

Li Yinhe's?

Don't need to. We have joint accounts.

I still haven't got over her.

I know. I told you, you could look at it simply. But I understand it was difficult. Thirty billion yuan, huh? You didn't sell yourself cheap.

No Chief, not cheap. May I unbutton my shirt?

Why the fuck?

They held me for two days. The days in April when I didn't report. They worked me over nicely.

I'm sorry to hear that. Don't show me your badge of courage.

What do we do now? It's a bit like that movie, which one was it?

Too many of them. I told Li Yinhe about it, the first time I ever told her anything like this. It's a pity. We talked about the good old days. The World Movie Appreciation course, everything. I didn't want it to end like this.

Chief, you seem to forget about my gun. For the first time, Wang Xiaobo noticed that Luo Xiaosi had a painting behind him, a strange one which showed two horsemen charging at each other with swords drawn.

True. Luo Xiaosi smiled. Only I don't plan to die right now. He looked straight into Wang Xiaobo's eyes.

Wang Xiaobo knew the moment had come. He looked into Luo Xiaosi's eyes. *Chief, about Luo Zi.*

Luo Xiaosi tensed.

Did you check? I think she's mine.

In the blankness which followed, Wang Xiaobo pointed at Luo Xiaosi's right wrist and squeezed the trigger twice. Then he aimed at the point between Luo Xiaosi's eyes and squeezed it again.

Luo Xiaosi's lips stretched, and his face seemed to light up. He stayed straight and looked back calmly. There was no blood. *It looks like they set you up.*

Wang Xiaobo looked at his gun, and then up again at Luo Xiaosi. He noticed the gap between Luo Xiaosi's eyebrows widen slowly. It took a while for the throbbing in Wang Xiaobo's head to die down.

You look shattered. Luo Xiaosi stayed stoic.

I shouldn't be. I guess you'll make it quick?

If I have to kill you, yes. But let me think this through.

If?

What's with the gun? Safety?

Wang Xiaobo stared hard at Luo Xiaosi.

Relax, no offence meant. Luo Xiaosi smiled. Let me think. He kept his gun pointed at Wang Xiaobo and sat down. *You know, I got a voice message from the Indian embassy today. Without an ID. A general who is ignorant of his enemy's situation is devoid of humanity.*

Why do you want me to know?

I don't, I'm thinking. I'm thinking this is LKY's way of warning me. He lowered his gun and slumped.

Wang Xiaobo had an idea. *I could...*

Luo Xiaosi snapped back to attention, the gun pointed at Wang Xiaobo's chest. *Okay,* he thought, *here's what we'll do. Make a call to your bank. Get the thirty billion transferred to this account. I'll tell you the account and the XFS code.*

I was about to suggest something similar. After that?

We'll see what to do with you.

I guess I should thank you.

No need. It didn't make sense. We tried our best. Some things didn't work because other things worked too well.

Luo Xiaosi?

Yes.

Wang Xiaobo hesitated. *Can I keep ten billion? You know...*

Luo Xiaosi sighed. *Keep five.*

Actually, I've spent one. He raised an arm. *Okay, Chief, don't look at me like that.* Wang Xiaobo followed his instructions. He had just finished when Luo Zi burst in. She was flushed and it broke Wang Xiaobo's heart when he recognised the signs.

'What's wrong?' she shouted first in spoken words. Then she calmed down and switched to the thought phone. *You called? What's all this? Guns in your hands? And you, Sir? You're crying?*

Wang Xiaobo nodded, wiping the tears with his sleeve. *It's okay now.*

Luo Xiaosi's thoughts floated across in a whisper. *I shouldn't pay you for today, because you weren't there when I needed you most.*

Luo Zi looked crushed.

Wang Xiaobo felt a warmth he had never felt before. She was looking at him. *Are you okay, Sir?*

He slumped. *I'm okay, yes, and about...*

She frowned in a puzzled kind of way. *It's all right.*

What? Luo Xiaosi was looking at them.

Forget it, Dad. And I'm sorry about, you know. She shrugged.

Get lost, before I fire you. Luo Xiaosi tried to put on a stern look, but it didn't work.

Wang Xiaobo realised he was hugging his own shoulders. He had left his gun on the table. *So, what now? Can I stay here? I want to talk to her.*

Luo Xiaosi ran his hand over his sparse hair. *No. Go back. They'll take it as a sign of peace. No more HCBB. You're banished. Screw around. You have four billion. Enjoy your life.* He sighed and got up.

You know, Luo Xiaosi, when I said she might be mine?

What about it?

It didn't suck up my energy like it should have. I think it's true. No shit.

Luo Xiaosi stretched and yawned. *Frankly my dear, I don't give a damn.*

Wang Xiaobo smiled a weak smile. He was still slouching. It had been too much for him. *I think this is the beginning of a beautiful new friendship.*

Glossary

ANTAKSHARI
Popular group game based on cinema songs

BAISAKH
Lunar month in summer

BURKHA
Arabic, enveloping outer garment; the veil can be pulled back to reveal the face.

CHAKRAVYUH
Specialised circular battle formation

CHANAKYA
A teacher, political scientist and economist. Advisor to the Mauryan emperor, Chandragupta (340–293 BCE).

DURYODHAN
The unconquerable one

GHAT
Stepped river bank

GURUKUL
Guru's establishment

HOURI
Arabic, beautiful companion

ISI
Directorate for Inter-Services Intelligence, the intelligence service of Pakistan.

JI

Suffix which serves as a mark of respect

KOTTAPAL

Police Officer

KRIYA

In the context used, sequence of yogic procedures

LAKSHMAN REKHA

A line of no return. In the epic *Ramayan*, Ram's brother Lakshman drew this line around the hut in which he left Sita alone and told Sita not to cross the line. Ravan tricked Sita into crossing the line and kidnapped her.

MALHOTRA

A family name

MAHURT

Forty-eight minutes

MATA

Mother

MULLAH

Urdu, religious cleric

NAXALITE

Militant rebel movement, in eastern and southern states of India, named after its village of origin

OM

Sanskrit, sacred exclamation

PADMA SHRI

Hindi, Indian civilian award

PIPAL

Ficus religiosa, sacred fig tree

RAJMATA

Queen Mother

SARI

Garment

SHO

Station House Officer, a police official

SAXENA

A family name

SHLOKA

Sanskrit/Hindi, sacred verse

SUYODHAN

Great warrior

Notes and Acknowledgments

I CANNOT RECALL ALL the sources I have drawn inspiration from. I do remember some very clearly. I got my first complete view of the *Mahabharat* from C.R. Rajagopalachari's translation.

Mukul corrected an error in a draft of 'Truth' and taught me a bit of what he knows about the process of writing. I borrowed, as I guess Mark Twain would put it, two ideas for 'Justice' and 'Honour'—one from a Lieutenant Boruvka story by Joseph Skvorecky, and the other from a novel by Keigo Higashino.

Vijay Mausi was kind enough to help me with the first line-by-line edit of 'The Trial.' The statement in this story about some people being worse than thieves is based on the quality philosophy of a Japanese engineer, Genichi Taguchi. For this story, I also used some information in public speeches by P. Sainath.

In 'Honour,' Virsa's explanation of locked room possibilities draws on the locked room lecture in John Dickson Carr's *The Hollow Man*. The statement about some people wanting us to do better than them was made by a professor at IIT Roorkee (then University of Roorkee). I developed a feel for the subject by reading the Hindi novel *Karn Ki Atmakatha* (*Karn's Autobiography*) by Manu Sharma, though I did not stick to Shri Sharma's storyline.

In 'The Meeting,' some of the lines used by meeting participants are from *The Art of War* (translated by Samuel B. Griffith), *Confucius from the Heart* by Yu Dan, *Monkey God* (translated by Arthur Waley) and *The Outlaws of the Marsh* (translated by Sidney Shapiro). At some points, there are references to system dynamics concepts created by Jay Forrester. I decided to take most of the names of characters in this story from the text of Wang Xiaobo's *Wang in Love and Bondage*. I also drew on some academic papers by Aniel Karnani and *Making India Work* by William Nanda Bissell. I would like to record that I wrote this story in 2009. I only inserted one substantial change later—a reference to the heartbreaking Nirbhaya case.

Desirée at Carve Literary Services helped me improve my manuscript drafts with her detailed reading and editorial advice. The defects that remain are there because there was only so much she could get me to do. Nolwen, Krishna and Sudeep read the manuscript and between them they ensured that it went through four final versions. I depended on Anand, Khalid and Rudro to read the proofs. Rajeev encouraged me to write when I had just started.

Zoya put her heart into the cover, and I think it shows.

Before I got a trickle of acceptances for my stories, my main boast was that my mother thinks I am a genius. My family has always been a pillar of support for me. I am grateful to my parents and to Meeta, Shreyas and Nolwen that I got this far. I could say that they made me what I am, but honestly, it's not their fault that I turned out this way.